Other Works by B. Heather Mantler
The King's Ransom
For Wealth and Glory
Closing the Portal

Committed to Her Enemy

Wasted Love

B. Heather Mantler

Mantler Publishing Prince George

ISBN: 1927507049
ISBN-13: 9781927507049

Library and Archives Canada Cataloguing in Publication

Mantler,B.Heather,1987-
Wasted love / B. Heather Mantler.

ISBN 978-1-927507-04-9

I. Title.

PS8626.A676W37 2013 C813'.6 C2013-901823-9

Dedicated to Librarians:

Clare Willis for putting my first "book" in the library. Ms. Williams for holding up the first Harry Potter book and saying anyone could write a book, even though I didn't believe it at the time. Mrs. Woollard for encouraging my reading. Sandra Jandric for encouraging both my reading and writing. Allan Wilson for helping with the story "Level P," as well as everything he does for the Prince George Public Library.

ZEBULON IS THE CURRENT KING AND HE IS IN LOVE WITH THE WOMAN HE CAN SEE OUT THE WINDOW

King Zebulon of Proster was the second king to rein after the destruction of the Batend army. It had been his father, Prince Proster of Grackle, who had invaded and defeated that army. King Proster had ruled over the kingdom of Proster for eight years before he found a wife, Ruana, among the populace. Zebulon was the oldest child with two younger sisters, Hertha and Narda. And they all lived happily until a demon showed up in the kingdom and started stealing children. Narda disappeared shortly before Proster rode off to battle the demon.

When Proster had returned with the children he looked like he had aged ten years. He never spoke of what happened to Narda. She was just gone, never to return, and without any reason given. Ruana had not taken the disappearance of her youngest child well and the fact that

Proster would not talk about what happened made things worse. The kingdom continued on as usual because Proster's advisors kept things going. After Hertha was married off to Lord Pardes of Grackle, Ruana had gone to live out at her family vineyard. Proster concentrated his world on running the kingdom.

Zebulon was not sure how Proster had even continued to on after all that, but he had. And he had taught Zebulon all that was necessary to be king. Then last year Proster became sick. The doctor had been called, but there was nothing anyone could do for him. He died within the month. Zebulon took the throne, but he was not sure that he was ready to become king. His father's advisors had continued in their positions to help Zebulon run the kingdom.

Now, King Zebulon was sitting on the throne, his chin resting on his palm with his elbow on the arm of the throne. Herwin was standing slightly behind the throne. In front of the dais was a crowd of nobles and diplomats all vying for his attention. His eyes had glazed over an hour ago and without Herwin nudging him every five minutes he might have fallen asleep.

Today all the diplomats from the nearby kingdoms were in court to discuss the treaties that Zebulon was supposed to be working to put in place, but he had been ignoring. No one had bothered his father was treaties because they figured he could just wipe them out if he wanted to. Now that he was dead and the army was of a slightly smaller size, they wanted treaties. They also hoped that Zebulon would be interested in marrying the princess from their kingdom. Zebulon had no interest in any of the portraits that had been brought to him, but Herwin and Garrick kept suggesting that he should not dismiss any of them. Zebulon dismissed them without a single thought or glance at the portraits. They would all be useful for fuelling fires around the castle.

The current total of diplomats in the kingdom was five. There was Atius, who was the diplomat from Lithimin. He was a tall thin man with one of those fancy mustaches that left people too busy staring at it to listen to what he was saying. Since that was his only visible hair it was even more prominent. It was black and stretched the width of his head. He used wax to keep it horizontal.

Jarlan was the diplomat from Grackle. He was a foot shorter than Zebulon, who was not much over five feet. He made up for it in width because the circumference of Jarlan was about ten feet. He had the ability to eat anything in sight and smell anything not in sight. Zebulon figured that Jarlan was sent out as a diplomat because Grackle could not afford to feed him.

Gaius was the diplomat for Sendal, which was between Grackle and Lithimin. Gaius was as thin as Jarlan was fat. He was skeletal and more than once been mistaken for a dead body. There were several people who avoided him because they were scared to catch whatever disease he had. Gaius had everything done for him by a man named Martin. Martin was a kindly young man, who was always cheerfully whistling down the hallways of the castle. He was helpful and always doing something useful. Gaius was never in a good mood and was always insulting Martin. Between the two of them, Zebulon figured that Gaius should have gone home and left Martin there to discuss the treaty.

The last neighbouring kingdom was Wodend and the diplomat was Luce. Luce wore a black cloak and glided rather than walked. He was always sneaking up on people. He liked dark corners and was the reason Zebulon had ordered that there never to be any shadows in his study. Luce was the only diplomat who did not make presentations to the court. He stood to one side and watched others do such things. He was merely there for when Zebulon was ready to discuss the treaty.

Myles was the diplomat for Jagel. Jagel was south beyond Wodend. Zebulon was not sure why Jagel had sent Myles to Proster. There was no trade between the two kingdoms and no other connections. The only reason that Myles might have for being sent to Proster and staying was the five portraits that he had brought with him. All the rest of the diplomats had brought one for Zebulon to consider for marriage, but Myles had five of them which he brought up at every possible convenience to the irritation of everyone else. Myles was always talking about romance, love and how the castle could use a woman's touch. As far as anyone could tell Myles was not married, but Zebulon would have been surprised if he did not leave some children in Proster when he went home to Jagel.

The others filling the throne room were nobles of Proster who would have liked to be the king's favourite. They all tried to do favours for him, entertain him, and get him to notice them. They showed up in the throne room as part of the court. Zebulon had no use for any of them. A group of able bodied men and women who dressed up to stand around the throne room all day always seemed to be a waste of resources to Zebulon, but nothing he could do stopped them from coming.

Of the few Zebulon did notice occasionally there was Clarinda, who was the daughter of Loic the captain of the guard. She was hoping to catch Zebulon's eye so that he would marry her. She had long blonde hair that she wore in ringlets and pink ribbons. She was always wearing fancy pink dresses. Zebulon had wondered, more than once, how Loic could afford his daughter's taste in clothing. According to the rumours, Clarinda had a lot of lovers all of whom were at least five years younger than she was.

The next member of court that was hard not to notice was Argus the son of Lord Breton. He was pudgy and really liked to wear feathers on things. It looked ridiculous, but he was always preening them. If Argus had been able to tell a joke he might have a made a good court jester, instead he just stood there and looked funny.

Zebulon did not know who Orestes' father was, or if he had any connection to nobility. Orestes just showed up one day in court and had not left. He was willing to fight anyone or anything that was put in front of him. He also had the muscles for it. His hair was naturally curly and orange. He was clean shaven and wore clothes that showed off his muscles.

Nasia was spending her time at court because she did not have anything else to do with her time. Her father was a member of the guard and her mother was of the nobility before Proster took over the kingdom. She was also the middle child of seven and thus not necessary for furthering the family's spot in society. But she also had money to do what she wanted. Nasia had a crush on Orestes, but was waiting for him to chase her. He had not noticed her yet, but she was starting to get desperate so that was going to change soon.

Then there was Dard. Dard was the son of the head cook, but no one besides Zebulon knew that. He knew because he and Dard had grown up together. The friendship had lasted quite well. Now Dard was popular among the people at court, which meant that Zebulon provided money to Dard and Dard brought information back to Zebulon. It worked well for both of them.

Zebulon was more likely to talk to Dard about his problems than Herwin and Garrick. Herwin and Garrick were more into giving advice than listening. There were plenty of others at court that Zebulon did not know quite so well.

Zebulon felt a sharp poke in his back. He straightened up as he blinked away his thoughts. Gaius had finished his presentation and everyone was looking at Zebulon expectantly. He let them wait in silence as he looked over the faces and finally settling back on Gaius.

"Was that it?" Zebulon asked.

"Yes, Your Majesty," Gaius answered.

"That was fascinating." Zebulon said, "You must give it again some time."

"Whenever you want, Your Majesty," Gaius said with a bow before backing into the group.

"Well?" Zebulon asked, "Who is next?"

"That was everyone, King Zebulon," Herwin answered. Zebulon could hear Herwin's teeth grinding in frustration.

"Then I guess that the court is dismissed," Zebulon said with an absent wave. Everyone bowed before filing out of the throne room.

"Your Majesty should try to pay attention to what the diplomats are saying," Herwin's voice was quiet so that no one but Zebulon could hear him. Zebulon did not respond to Herwin.

The last person left the throne room and the door was left open. Zebulon stood up and stepped off the dais. Herwin started to follow him. Zebulon turned and glared at him. Herwin stopped and stayed where he was as Zebulon turned back around and headed out of the throne room. The hallway outside the throne room was empty as everyone else had gone out to the courtyard. They would not head home yet because they wanted to make sure that Zebulon would not call the court together again today. They did not want to miss court for fear that they might not be let back in or something.

Zebulon walked through the hallways and every time he passed a servant they bowed or curtsied to him so that their faces were to the ground. His father would have gotten upset with them and told them that he would rather see their faces than the top of their heads. Zebulon just continued past without glancing at the servants. He had more important things to do than yell at servants for doing what they have been taught to do.

Zebulon reached the staircase that went up to the highest tower of the castle and started to climb. The staircase started at the main floor of the castle and went all the way up without stopping. The first time Zebulon had climbed it he had not made it half way before he headed back down out of tiredness. Now he had no trouble going up at a good pace. It also kept him from gaining weight from all the food he ate.

At the top of the staircase was a wooden door with a bar across it and a symbol carved into the wood. He had never tried to open, but he knew his father had put the symbol there to stop people from opening the door. There were many things in the castle his father had never told him about until the summer before he died. The castle had several places to hide treasure. How Proster and his men had found them all when he had attacked and taken over the castle, Zebulon had no idea. They all seemed so well hidden. Proster had not told Zebulon what was behind the door at the top of the staircase, but Zebulon had never told his father about coming up here.

Beside the door was a window which overlooked the whole city. Zebulon stopped in front of the window and rested his elbows on the sill. It was the middle of the afternoon and the city was bustling with activity. The sounds of the market could be heard all the way up here. The smell was also brought to him by the wind.

Zebulon ignored all that and took out his spyglass. He put it to his eye and searched the market place for the stall he wanted. It took a minute, but he found it.

The stall was run by two women, one older and one younger. They sold a small amount of vegetables, probably whatever they grew in their own garden. Few people bought from them and usually it was the same people who had bought from them before. The older woman had long silver hair, solid frame, and ragged clothing that was too big. The young woman had a similar frame, but was thinner. Her clothing was ragged as well, but it fit better. She also had long hair that was black. Zebulon also knew that her eyes were bright blue and full of worries.

Zebulon had seen her one day while riding through the city in his carriage. He had been tucked safely away as Herwin wanted and was staring out the window at all the people who were going about their business unconcerned about whose carriage was going passed. The women had set up their stall just outside the market place and the younger one was calling for buyers. Her soft voice had sounded over all other noise coming from the market to him and the sudden need came over him to see the owner of such a voice. He had gotten closer to the window and looked out. She was not hard to spot among the crowd. At the sight of her, Zebulon's heart had sped up, warmth spread over his chest, and for the first time in his life he felt alive. His whole body had cried out for her. He wanted to call for the driver to stop. He wanted to get out of the carriage and go over to her. He wanted to offer her the world and anything else she wanted. He wanted to tell her that she had captured his heart at a glance. He wanted to invite her and her mother into the carriage and up to the castle to live the rest of their lives in comfort. He wanted to announce his love for her to the world. But he just watched her as the carriage rolled on passed. Once she was out of sight he had moved back in the seat and went back to staring out the window.

The feelings had never left him. The only difference was the longing for her in his mind. So, he came up her with his spyglass to watch her as she and her mother tried to sell vegetables. He had no idea what her name was, or who she was, or where she lived, or anything else about her. He supposed that he could find the information. He could also go down to the market and approach her. He had gone to the market without the carriage and security before, but those trips were rare and there had to be a very important reason for it. Zebulon also had not told anyone about his feelings for the woman. Herwin and Garrick would probably tell him to forget her and pick one of the women at court. Dard would tell him to go to her and at least get her name. But to bring her to court would make her life harder. She would be bullied and harassed by those who already made the court their territory. She would be looked down on by those of noble background. Zebulon did not want her life to be harder just because of who he was.

Zebulon had heard the story of how his father had seen his mother in the market place and fallen in love with her. Proster found out who she was and begged her father for her hand in marriage. She moved into the castle and had lived there until her oldest daughter was married. But things had been simpler back then. There were no nobles that spent time in court. There were no advisors who believed that marriage should be on the same social level. He just had to find her and marry her. Zebulon could not do that without it creating other problems.

The sounds of someone coming up the stairs came to Zebulon. Reluctantly he removed the spyglass from his eye and closed it before putting it away. He did not want anyone knowing what exactly he was doing up here. It was better that they think he was just staring out at the city. The foot falls were getting closer and Zebulon could now hear the person panting. It was not a servant that was coming up, but someone who was not used to stairs. Servants came up here to clean occasionally or to let him know that he was needed elsewhere. None of them had any problems with the stairs.

Zebulon glanced over as the person came into sight. It was Dard. He was sweating, panting and his legs looked ready to give out. He came to the spot beside Zebulon and collapsed against the wall. He slid to the ground and stayed there. Zebulon continued to look out over the city and did not say anything to Dard. Dard worked to get his breathing under control to talk.

Without the spyglass it was impossible to see what was going on in the city below. It was just buildings and streets. There were no people or individuality. It would be easy to rule from up here without the worry of how it would affect the people. But Zebulon knew that was not how a king should rule. The further from the people the harder it was to know when they were in need. At the present, the people were satisfied with their lives and there was very little that Zebulon could do for the people. The diplomats were here to make treaties to prevent wars, but really there was not much chance of one being started. The kingdom of Proster was self-sufficient and really did not need any trading agreements.

"How do you get up here?" Dard was starting to get his breath back.

"I do it about once per day." Zebulon answered, "That keeps me in good enough condition that I do not end up like you."

"That explains why you do not gain weight despite all that you eat," Dard said.

Zebulon did not respond, but continued to look out the window. Dard slowly got to his feet and rested his forearms on the window sill

"Up here surveying your kingdom?" Dard asked.

"I have to remember why I am the king." Zebulon replied, "Otherwise I might end up as one of those kings who does not remember that there is a world outside the walls of the castle."

"So, who is she?" Dard asked, "And how do you see her from here?"

"She and her mother run a stall in the market place," Zebulon answered, "and I can see her with this." He took the spyglass out of his pocket and showed it to Dard. Dard took the spyglass and extended it before putting it to his eye.

"It is amazing how far you can see with this thing." Dard said as he scanned the market place, "Which one is she?"

"Near the north entrance on the right, fourth stall in," Zebulon answered. Dard focused where Zebulon told him and did not say anything as he studied what he found.

"She is good looking." Dard said, "I can see her as your type. Why do you not go down and introduce yourself, rather than stay up here and watch her?"

"Too much opposition if I announced that I was marrying a peasant," Zebulon said.

"You are the king." Dard said, "If you want to marry a peasant, nothing should get in your way. The people do not care, or will go the other way and be all for it. If you let the supposed nobility and those two advisors rule your life, you will never have any happiness for yourself. And you deserve some happiness. Go down and talk to her."

"I will think about." Zebulon said taking the spyglass back from Dard, "Was there a reason you came up to see me?"

"You are going to have some problems with the diplomats." Dard said, "I have not been able to get the specifics, but three of them are in on a scheme to kill you."

"I do not see much point in killing me." Zebulon said, "It is not like they will be able to take the throne and start ruling Proster. Although I suppose that part of this plan comes from the kingdoms of origin, not the diplomats themselves."

"Who does get the throne should you die?" Dard asked.

"My sister, Hertha," Zebulon answered, "she would have to come back from Grackle and take the throne."

"Then Jarlan is likely to be part of it." Dard said, "They could put Hertha on the throne and rule through her, or have her give Proster to Grackle. It would mean that they could get the kingdom without having to destabilize it and keep the money flowing straight to them without interruption."

"Hertha would not be bothered about ruling it, so most likely the king of Grackle would take things over." Zebulon said, "The question just remains who else is in on it and what do they expect to get from it? Also how do they plan to kill me?"

"I am still looking for all that information," Dard said, "but I figured that it would be best to warn you about all of this. I am trying to get as many sources of information as I can without being caught."

"I will be watchful for attacks on my person." Zebulon said, "I should also see if I can find information about what is going on in the neighbouring kingdoms. If I know where they are at politically and economically then I should have a better idea of who will want to take me out."

"Luce seems like one of the other people in on the plan." Dard said, "He gives me an eerie sensation whenever I notice him."

"There are five diplomats." Zebulon said, "You said three have a plan. I admit that Luce seems very likely to be in on the plan, but we need to know for certain. I cannot do anything against them until I know for certain which ones."

"You need to go down and talk to the girl." Dard said, "If there are two people in the bed, one of them might hear an intruder."

"I will talk to her when I am ready." Zebulon said, "Not to use her for an alarm. She does not deserve that kind of treatment."

"Would you like me to see what I find about her?" Dard asked.

"No." Zebulon answered, "When I am ready I will do all that myself."

"Very well," Dard said.

They stood in silence for several minutes as they watched the sun move across the sky and the effects of that on the buildings below.

"Is there a girl out there for you?" Zebulon asked.

"I hope so," Dard answered, "but I very much doubt that she would be truly interested in me."

"Who is she?" Zebulon asked.

"Thalia." Dard answered, "She is one of the ladies who comes to court."

"I thought you had all those ladies wrapped around your finger," Zebulon said.

"She is very worried about status and possessions." Dard replied, "If she does not know where a person stands she avoids them. I get by with dressing fashionably, but that is not enough for her. She is lovely, if a bit shallow, and I wish she would notice me, but she does not know where I stand, so I am not within her circle or interest."

"So, you need a title to go along with the pretty clothes," Zebulon said.

"If I want to be noticed by her," Dard said, "but I am not of the nobility and thus do not have the worries of being a nobleman."

"I will think about it." Zebulon said, "Probably after all the treaties are signed and the diplomats are shipped off."

"You need to start the negotiations soon," Dard said, "and sleeping while they are talking is not going to get those negotiations done."

"It was just so boring I could not help myself," Zebulon said, "but I will try again tomorrow."

"Good." Dard said, "If you will excuse me, I have a party to go to."

"You are excused," Zebulon said, "be careful going down the stairs."

"I will," Dard said before turning and heading back down the stairs. Zebulon did not watch him go, but took the spyglass out and searched for the market stall and the woman who owned his heart.

PLAYING POLITICS BY LEARNING CONDITIONS IN OTHER KINGDOMS AND AVOIDING ASSASSINS

The sky was starting to darken when Zebulon could hear someone coming up the stairs. He had put away the spyglass half an hour ago because the woman and her mother had packed up their stall and gone home, so he did not have to put that way. The sound of the footsteps suggested that the person was familiar with the stairs and most likely to be a servant. Zebulon did not change his position or take his eyes off the city. The lights were starting to come on in the houses and made interesting patterns from this distance.

Finally the servant came into sight and stopped at the top of the stairs. He was slightly out of breath, but otherwise fine. He bowed to Zebulon.

"Yes?" Zebulon asked.

"Supper is served," the servant reported.

"I will take mine in my study," Zebulon replied.

"Yes, Sire," the servant said before straightening up and heading back down the stairs. Zebulon waited by the window until he could no longer hear the footfalls of the servant before he started down the stairs.

When Zebulon reached his office, his supper was on the desk and no one was there. Zebulon sat down in his chair and brought the tray closer to himself along with the papers from the lower court. He picked up and studied the complaint before absently reaching for his fork. He picked it up and was about to stick it into the potatoes when suddenly Zebulon saw this white wolf in front of him. He dropped both fork and paper as he caused his chair to fall back. The chair hit the floor with a thud and Zebulon remained in it. He stayed still for several minutes. Nothing happened in that time. Slowly Zebulon untangled himself from the chair and stood up. His office was the same as it had before. No one else was there and there was no wolf. His fork was lying on the tray and the paper had fallen to the floor. Zebulon picked up the paper and placed it on the desk.

He moved around the office, but found no trace of any wolf. Finally he sat down in his chair again. Zebulon shook his head as he picked up his fork. He was not sure why his brain had brought up an image of a wolf, but it was gone now and he could get on with his supper. This time he cut up a piece of meat and started to bring a piece to his mouth. The wolf was right there in front of him and growling in his face. Zebulon dropped the fork and the wolf disappeared.

Zebulon did another check of his office and found no trace of the wolf. He sat down again and looked at his tray. He put the fork back on the plate and pushed it away from him. Zebulon moved the pile of paper closer and started to go through them. The wolf did not reappear.

Zebulon was blinking to keep himself awake. He had read through all the complaints and added comments to the ones he thought needed comments. He had started to read the suggested treaty that Jarlan had brought with him. Zebulon was having trouble staying awake reading the same thing he had had trouble staying awake while listening to. Whoever wrote it had no sense of interesting and was all about political language. Great for a sleep aid, but useless for a treaty. What Zebulon could read of it had several items he considered rude to even suggest that he would give that away.

There was a knock at the door. He looked up with a puzzled expression. It was late enough at night that most people had gone to bed and his supper tray had been removed hours ago. Zebulon picked up the dagger that he used as a letter opener and slid it up his sleeve before bringing his hands to his lap.

"Come in," Zebulon called. The door opened and the head cook entered carrying a lantern. His hands were shaking and his face was white.

"Yes?" Zebulon asked.

"Excuse me, Your Majesty," the head cook said, "but are you feeling well this evening?"

"I am feeling fine," Zebulon said.

"That is good," the head cook said.

"What happened?" Zebulon asked.

"The dog who ate the remains of your supper died ten minutes ago." the head cook answered, "It was not sick before it ate."

"I am sorry to hear about the dog." Zebulon said, "I was not hungry and did not eat any supper."

"Would you like me to employ a taster?" the head cook asked.

"No," Zebulon answered, "I will take all my meals in the dining room from now on and eat out of the same pot as everyone else."

"Yes, Your Majesty," the head cook bowed and then left the office. His face did not look as pale when he closed the door.

Zebulon refused the request to hold court the next day, but did sit in his throne room to do his paperwork. The door to the throne room was left open for those who wished to speak with him.

It was mid-morning when Herwin entered the throne room and closed the door behind him.

"What can I do for you this morning, Herwin?" Zebulon asked.

"I wish to speak to you about the treaties," Herwin answered.

"Yes, I have been trying to read up on them," Zebulon said pointing to a pile of papers near his hand, "But they are very complicated, are they not?"

"The kingdom of Proster does not need any trade with the neighbouring kingdoms." Herwin said, "Perhaps it is best if you sent the diplomats home and just arrange for a gathering of the kings. It would be better for communication."

"I hardly think that is necessary." Zebulon said, "The diplomats are doing their best and they are entertaining. They are such good people, why would I want to rush them home?"

"Zebulon," Herwin's voice was fatherly, "the welfare of the kingdom is at stake. Their entertainment value is not worth losing your kingdom over."

"They are here to arrange treaties, not taking my kingdom away from me." Zebulon said, "You are just being paranoid, they will not do any harm."

"Zebulon," Herwin tried again.

"That is King Zebulon," Zebulon put irritation into his voice, "and you are an advisor, that is all. As king I have decided they should be allowed to stay. That is my final decision."

"Yes, Your Majesty," Herwin bowed before leaving the throne room. Zebulon wondered how his father ever kept Herwin and Garrick in line. They never seemed to bother Proster or give him endless advice like they did with Zebulon. Herwin was slightly easier to push away, but Garrick would not have backed down without a bigger fight. Zebulon was sure that they both meant well, but they were likely to run the kingdom into the ground and destroy his life. Sending the diplomats home now would result in insulting the kingdoms. Then they were more likely to start a war. Zebulon did not want to get involved in a war, because he did not want the people to suffer over some power hungry king. They have not done anything to deserve that. It would be better to leave this between him and the diplomats. There would be fewer causalities that way.

Someone cleared their throat. Zebulon looked up and saw Jarlan was standing before the dais. Zebulon was going to have to pay more attention to his surroundings.

"What is it that you wish to talk to me about?" Zebulon asked.

"Have you had time to look over the treaty, King Zebulon?" Jarlan asked.

"I have," Zebulon answered, "just recently, but I do not understand some of the wording. Perhaps you can explain parts of it to me."

"I can try," Jarlan said.

"There is a chair over there, bring it over," Zebulon pointed to the chair that was beside the door to the throne room. Jarlan walked over to it and dragged it back to just below the dais. Once it was placed he sat down in it.

"What is the first thing that confuses you, King Zebulon?" Jarlan asked once he was comfortable.

"This first sentence says, Grackle combined," Zebulon said, "last I heard it was all one kingdom."

"The kingdom has been divided into Lordoms." Jarlan replied, "As such all of the lords have a voice in decisions made by the crown."

"That must be an awfully complicated process." Zebulon said, "What if you need to make a decision in an emergency and no one is at court?"

"Grackle has not been making decisions without all the lords having their say in the matter," Jarlan replied.

"Too complicated," Zebulon said, "however did such a mess come about?"

"After Proster left, there was a gathering of the lords," Jarlan said, "and they decided that King Alaric was not fit to rule. To prevent a takeover from another kingdom they decided to divide up the land into Lordoms. Each lord was responsible for feeding, defending, and ruling over their part. The king would be more of a figure head than an actual person in authority."

"Is Alaric's son the king?" Zebulon asked.

"No, Alaric took his family to the summer home and never returned to the castle, or the throne." Jarlan answered, "The current king is the son of King Thedious's top advisor. He willingly took the position of king with the knowledge that there was little to no power attached to it. It has worked well thus far. So, in the treaty combined merely means that all the lords agree. What is the next part you wish to ask about?"

Before Zebulon could ask another question, the castle steward entered the throne room.

"Yes?" Zebulon asked.

"Lunch is ready, Your Majesty," the steward replied.

"Thank you." Zebulon said as he stood up, "Will you be joining us for lunch, Jarlan?"

"I will," Jarlan said as he got to his feet. Zebulon led the way out of the throne and into the dining room. Zebulon sat at the head table and Jarlan sat at one of the lower tables.

After lunch was over, Zebulon went back and sat in the throne room. No one bothered him. Jarlan did not even come back to discuss the rest of the terms of the treaty with him. About the middle of the afternoon, Zebulon left the throne room and went up the stairs to the tower. It took him several minutes to scan the market place for the stall. He did not see or it was not there. Either way, Zebulon felt the loss as he put the spyglass away. But he did not go back down stairs. There was no one waiting to see him and there was nothing else he had to do. Currently he was not needed for anything.

Zebulon went up to his bedroom after he had gone over any other paperwork that was required of him for the day. He stripped down and crawled into bed. His eyes closed and he was asleep.

The trees were so tall that it was impossible to see the top of them. The brush was knee height and grew everywhere, except the path on which Zebulon was standing. He could not see anything more than a few feet in front of him and for some unknown reason could not turn to look behind him. His feet kept him walking along this path. He walked along it for a long time without seeing anything, or coming upon anything. It was just forest that went on forever. Zebulon had dreamed this forest before. It never ended and there was nothing else here. Why his mind brought this place up, he did not know.

Suddenly standing in the middle of the path was a white wolf with bright blue eyes. It looked at him and he stopped in his tracks. He had seen the wolf the day before, but he had not seen it in his dream before. The wolf studied him as he studied it. There was no expression in its eyes and it fur was white without even dirt on it.

"You are in danger," a voice drifted to Zebulon. He could not tell if it was male or female, but he thought it might have come from the wolf.

"Danger from what?" Zebulon asked.

"The assassin," the wolf answered, "He is entering your bed chamber. You must wake up now."

"Who, or what, are you?" Zebulon asked.

"Wake up, now!"

The wolf was gone and the forest had disappeared. The darkness was only broken by the light of the moon that was coming in the window. Zebulon slid the hand that was closest to his head under his pillow. He could not hear anyone else moving, or breathing, but he could sense the person was there. Zebulon carefully looked around without moving his head. There was the shadow of a man standing by the door. Zebulon felt his hand wrap around the handle of the dagger that he kept under his pillow. Then he closed his eyes again and laid still. He controlled his breathing to make it regular and deep.

Slowly he sensed the man getting closer to the bed. The man moved without a sound as he crept closer. He moved and then stopped to study Zebulon for movement. When Zebulon did not move, he inched closer. Zebulon waited until the man was not far from the bed. Then he sat up and stabbed the man in the abdomen. The man was shocked and did not react as Zebulon pulled the dagger out. The man did not fall either and Zebulon stabbed him again. Slowly the man collapsed to the rug. Zebulon lit the candle beside his bed. The man, who was now bleeding to death on the rug, was unfamiliar to him. Zebulon reached down and pulled the dagger out. He used it to cut the man's throat and end his suffering.

Then Zebulon got out of bed being careful of the corpse lying in the carpet. He went to the wardrobe and pulled out some clothes. He quickly slipped into the clothes. Zebulon went back to the man. The man's blood was still dripping from his throat. Zebulon pulled the rug over the man and wrapped him in it.

Zebulon went to the door of his room and looked out in the hallway. There was no one in sight. Zebulon opened the door all the way. He went back to the rug and pulled it out into the hallway. He dragged the rug down the hallway. Zebulon went along the hallway to what his father called the 'back door.' The door was in the back of castle and anyone who went through it fell to their deaths.

It would be a good place to deal with the assassin without alerting anyone about it. Zebulon arrived and unlocked the door before opening it. He pushed the body and rug over the edge. Zebulon closed and locked the door. He headed back to his room.

He was just about there when he came upon the steward, who was holding a lantern up and looking around.

"Is there something wrong?" Zebulon asked the steward.

"No," the steward answered, "I was just doing my last check for the night and noticed your door open."

"I am fine." Zebulon said, "You can go to bed."

"Yes, Your Majesty," the steward said.

"Oh, and the rug from my room has gone missing." Zebulon said, "Can you find a replacement?"

"First thing in the morning, Your Majesty," the steward said with a bow.

"Good night," Zebulon said.

"Good night, Your Majesty," the steward said. Zebulon left the steward looking confused and went into his room. He closed the door behind him. He put the bar across the door before going through his room searching to see if anyone else was hiding in there. He did not find anything, so he stripped down again and climbed into bed. He stared up at the ceiling for a long time before his heart had slowed down to normal. Then he fell asleep.

Zebulon was trying to stay awake as Atius made a presentation that had to do with the treaty with Lithimin. The whole court was standing there watching him with a lot more interest than Zebulon was. Atius was not any more interesting than Jarlan. Both of them stood there and talked in a monotone voice. It was perfect cure for insomnia. Every time Zebulon tried to follow what Atius was saying his attention drifted off to other things.

Zebulon refocused on Atius and found him talking about all the great trading opportunities.

"Is there anything interesting happening in Lithimin besides trading stuff?" Zebulon interrupted Atius. Atius looked up in surprise. It was like he had fallen asleep to his own voice and had not noticed until now.

"There are lots of other things happening in Lithimin," Atius said.

"Like what?" Zebulon asked.

"Well," Atius started and then paused.

Zebulon waited for him to think.

"We have a very large timber industry," Atius finally found something, "but we have not been trading timber with our neighbours because we have been using all of the wood ourselves."

"Really?" Zebulon straightened up in his throne and dropped his hand to the arm of the throne, "What are you building?"

"Churches." Atius answered, "Since the king has welcomed the cardinal to the court, the focus of the kingdom has been on building churches and spreading the message of the church to all parts of the kingdom."

"My mother took me to church as I grew up." Zebulon said, "I have not gone in a long time. Your king must be strong in his belief."

"My king is ill of health and hopes belief will cure him." Atius said, "The cardinal has used it to help the church."

"At least it is for a good cause." Zebulon said, "Is there anything else of interest happening in Lithimin?"

"The main industry, aside from timber, is corn," Atius said, "especially where the trees have been cut down, there are fields upon fields of corn. Enough to supply everyone in three kingdoms is grown each year."

"Timber, church and corn." Zebulon said, "It does not sound like you do much of interest in a year."

Before Atius could respond the steward arrived to announce lunch. Zebulon got down from his throne and the rest followed him to the dining room.

After lunch, Zebulon went up to the tower and looked out the window with his spyglass. Today spotting the stall was easy and he could easily watch the woman. She was wearing the same rags as the last time he saw her, but somehow she looked more beautiful than she had before. Like her absence in his life had made him want her even more. His arms longed to hold her, his lips craved her kisses, and his life seemed empty without her. But his feet never moved any closer and his head continued to tell him that bringing her into his life would be a bad thing. Right now he had three diplomats trying to kill him and he did not know which of the five those were. It was not a situation to bring someone into if there is to be any hope of forever with them.

She was better off down there where she was safe from the intrigues of court. One day, when he thought it was safe, he would go down and talk to her. He would learn her name and her situation. Then he would fall to one knee and beg her to marry him. He would promise her forever in his life. He would explain that she already had his heart and that was the only thing he had that was worth anything. He could give her anything she wanted, but all he needed was her love. That was the only thing he longed for.

Zebulon had been told how his mother had been surprised at Proster's proposal and yet when she looked into his eyes it had felt right. She felt that this was the man for her to marry and that there was love in her heart for him. Zebulon hoped that the woman would see the same thing and feel the same way. He knew she would not jump into his arms immediately, but that was okay. He had people around him that would do that if he gave them a chance and that was not what he was looking for. None of the people around him would love him if he married them and lived with them for a thousand years. They were just there to get what they wanted from him.

Zebulon thought of his sister. She had married a nobleman from Grackle. His name had been Selby and he was a minor noble with a small estate between the kingdom of Proster and the capital of Grackle. Hertha had met Selby at church one Sunday while he was in Proster as a trade envoy. He had asked for her hand in marriage and it was granted after some thought. Zebulon's father had asked Hertha whether she loved him and wanted to marry him. Hertha said she wanted to marry him, but would not say if she loved him or not. Zebulon did not believe that Hertha loved Selby, especially since there had been reports of a son born a mere seven months after the wedding. Hertha had moved to Grackle by then and there was nothing anyone could do. The trade envoy got nothing as far trade or treaties, just a nobleman married to Hertha.

Zebulon's father had told him once that the curse of being of dwarven blood was that they fell in love with one person and there was no love truer than that one. Zebulon had found his in the market place, just as his father had, but Hertha had not. Zebulon wondered what would happen if she did find her true love. Would she have an affair on her husband? Would she deny herself the love? Would she be horrified at what she had done? Zebulon could not see himself marrying anyone, aside from the woman down there selling vegetables in the market place. She had his heart and she was his true love. True love meant they were supposed to be together and nothing would get in the way of that.

Each diplomat had brought a portrait of a lady to tempt Zebulon into marrying the princesses from those kingdoms. Zebulon had not been tempted by their beauty, or the stories of how great they were. He had found his true love before the diplomats had arrived. There was not going to be a treaty based in marriage, if there were any treaties at all. Zebulon knew that the treaties should be made to prevent war, but the discussion of what they could trade with Proster was more foolishness than reality. The kingdom of Proster was fine without any help and wanted none of what was offered. The people cared nothing for trading, except what they already did, but Zebulon had no business it that and did not care to get involved. They did not need his help.

The women packed up the few vegetables they had not sold and left the market place. Zebulon watched them until he could not see them anymore. Then he closed his spyglass and put it into his pocket. He watched the world go by for a little while longer. He could not see the people, but there was the sense that the world was going by, busy with its own things.

As if sensing the servant coming up to tell him it was supper time, Zebulon headed down the stair case. He met the servant half way down. The servant delivered the message and they both went the rest of the way down the stairs. Zebulon headed to the dining room for supper.

After spending most of his evening in his study, Zebulon went up to his bed chamber. He noticed the new rug in the place that the old one had been as he closed and locked the door. Zebulon walked through his room and looked carefully for signs of anymore assassins. He also checked for any traps that were supposed to kill him. He did not find any. Zebulon barred the door before stripping and climbing into bed. He snuffed the candle and closed his eyes. He was asleep shortly after.

Zebulon had not called his court to listen to another presentation. He sat on his throne and read a book. Supposedly people could come in and talk to him, but anyone who entered the throne room was ignored in favour of the book. At lunch, Zebulon took a break to eat in the dining room. After lunch, Zebulon went back to the throne room and his book. Again no one disturbed him, until the middle of the afternoon when Jarlan came into the throne room. Jarlan stood in front of the dais for several minutes waiting to be noticed and acknowledged. Then he gently cleared his throat to get Zebulon's attention. A few minutes later, Jarlan cleared his throat louder. He waited for several more minutes.

"Your Majesty?" Jarlan asked. Zebulon glared at him over the book.

"What do you want?" Zebulon snapped.

"I was wondering if you had considered the treaty any further," Jarlan replied, "I can answer any other questions you have."

"You had your chance to answer my questions the other day." Zebulon said curtly, "I am thinking about what you told me and what I understand from my reading. There is nothing more to discuss until I am ready."

"Yes, Your Majesty." Jarlan said, "If I might ask, when will that be?"

"No, you may not ask." Zebulon said, "You are dismissed."

"Yes, Your Majesty," Jarlan's response was filled with frustration. He bowed and left the throne room. Zebulon went back to his book.

After supper, Zebulon went into his study and sat down in his chair. He had just started going through the pile of paper work that had gathered over the course of the day, when there came a knock at the door.

"Come," Zebulon called. The door opened and Dard stepped into the study before closing the door behind him. Dard sat down in the chair across from Zebulon.

"What have you heard?" Zebulon asked.

"Jarlan is upset with you." Dard answered, "He is ready to have you dead and someone else in your place."

"I asked him about the current state of Grackle." Zebulon said, "It sounds like it is fractured."

"But there is a plan for one of the lords to take it over." Dard said, "Jarlan is working with that lord. The problem is that they do not have the army or the supplies to make the rest of the lords give up control. They need Proster to get those things and you are standing in their way."

"And Jarlan is getting help from two others for this plot?" Zebulon asked.

"I just cannot figure out which two." Dard answered, "I have not been able to catch them getting together to plan anything. Jarlan is losing patience so he is getting more vocal about the lack of a treaty. He is going to make that a point of contention and you have been helping that along."

"I do not want to deal with the treaty just yet, especially if there is a plot to kill me," Zebulon said, "because that would give them reasons to leave and then things would get farther out of control. Also if he gets too impatient, he might tell us more than he intends."

"He already is telling us more than he ever planned on." Dard said, "I will be keeping an eye on him."

"Atius talked about what was going on in his kingdom," Zebulon said, "Have you found out anything there?"

"Most of what he said is true." Dard said, "They are using the wood to build churches. The cardinal is running the kingdom because the king pretty much gave him the power. They have an overabundance of corn that they need to sell so that they can buy supplies to feed their people for the winter."

"Why not just feed the people corn?" Zebulon asked, "Or grow something that the people can eat for the winter?"

"The cardinal has decided that to trade with the neighbouring kingdoms, they need corn." Dard answered, "I do not think he is worried about feeding the people of that kingdom over the winter. I do not think he is worried about feeding them at all. There are many places where the people do not like the church interfering with their lives. Some corners of the kingdom have destroyed the church building that was put up. The buildings were burned and the priests run out. This upsets the cardinal, so he sends the guards to get the corn and leaves the place with only what they grew in their own gardens. What is rarely enough for one family to live and definitely not enough to share with those who do not have gardens. If the people without food have converted to the church and were not among those who wanted the church gone, then they are moved to a place where there is plenty of food for the winter."

"Would getting rid of me help them in anyway?" Zebulon asked.

"If they had too much corn and Grackle needs food supplies, then I would say yes." Dard answered, "It is likely that Atius is in on the plot."

"Have you found out anything else?" Zebulon asked.

"Not yet," Dard answered, "although there has been some surprise that you are still alive."

"My food was poisoned one night." Zebulon replied, "I did not eat any of it, but the dog who was fed the leftovers did and died from them. I also woke to find an assassin in my room the other night, but he was also dealt with. I have not told anyone about these incidents because I do not want anyone to know who does not already. Your father knows about the poisoning, but I did not explain the why, or anything else. I do not think it would be helpful to my position to tell people about the attempts on my life."

"As long as you survive them," Dard said.

"Anything else?" Zebulon asked.

"Nothing that I have found," Dard answered.

"How are relations with Thalia?" Zebulon asked.

"Warming," Dard answered, "I had one of her friends introduce us. She has noticed me, but I do not think it will go much farther until she has confirmed that I am not some imposter hoping to mingle with nobility."

"You will figure out what to do," Zebulon said, "and she will warm to you a little more."

"Not until you acknowledge me as something other than just another person hanging around the court for the prestige," Dard said.

"I have to figure out what titles are out there to give you," Zebulon replied, "and I do not have time to think at the moment."

"I know," Dard said as he got to his feet, "Good night."

"Good night," Zebulon said. Dard left the study and Zebulon started working on the pile of paper work.

It was late when Zebulon left his study and headed up to his room. As he walked he could hear someone moving behind him. There was a slight squeaking of the man's shoes on the floor. Zebulon looked behind him, but did not see anyone back there. The shadows in the halls were deep with only a few torches on the walls lit. A man on a horse could be creeping up on him and Zebulon would have trouble seeing them. Zebulon did not speed up, but let his senses inform him of the man following him.

The man stayed the same distance behind him all the way down the hallway, up the stairs and as Zebulon got closer to his bed chamber. When Zebulon reached the door to his bed chamber the man sped up. Zebulon turned from the door in time to see the knife in the light of the torch. He grabbed the wrist of the man before the knife could reach him. Zebulon snapped the man's wrist forcing the man to drop the knife. The knife clattered to the floor as the man cried out in pain.

The man reached out with his other hand and scratched Zebulon's arm with something. Zebulon grabbed the man's other wrist and smacked it hard against the wall. The man struggled to get his wrist free. Zebulon hit his head into the man's chin. The man's head smacked into the wall and he collapsed on to the ground. Zebulon let the man go. He looked over the man and found him unconscious. Zebulon took a deep breath.

Footsteps could be heard coming down the hallway. Then the steward came into sight.

"Are you all right?" the steward asked Zebulon when he saw the man lying on the floor.

"I think so," Zebulon said as he pulled his sleeve up and look at the scratch on his arm. It was not very deep and it did not look unhealthy.

"I will call the guard," the steward said as he turned to go back down the hallway.

"Do not," Zebulon's voice was firm. The steward stopped.

"Sire?" the steward asked.

"I do not want anyone to know what happened." Zebulon said, "Help me move him."

"All right, Your Majesty," the steward said as he came back to where Zebulon was.

"Take his feet." Zebulon said, "We are going to take him to the dungeon."

"Yes, Sire," the steward said as he bent down and picked up the man's feet. Zebulon picked up the man's wrists. They carried the man through the hallways to the door of the dungeon. There was no one else up, so they did not meet anyone else. The steward set down the man's ankles and opened the door. Then they carried the man down the stairs. There were only a few prisoners in the first handful of cells. They went passed all of those and into the second area of the dungeon. They dropped the man on to one of the torture tables and strapped him down.

"Is there anything else, sire?" the steward asked looking a little uncertain about the situation.

"No," Zebulon said, "just make sure that the dungeon master knows to feed him."

"Yes, Sire," the steward said before leaving. Zebulon looked over the man in the light of the torches he had lit. The man had no distinguishing features and nothing in his pockets to identify him. Zebulon left the man there and went back up to the hallway outside his room. He picked up the knife and the fighting star. Then he opened his door and went inside. Zebulon searched the room for any people or traps. When he was sure that it was safe, he locked and barred the door. He stripped down and crawled into bed. Sleep came to him quickly.

Gaius stood in the throne room and was giving his presentation. He was trying to keep Zebulon interested. Every time Zebulon's eyes glazed over, Gaius would say something loud, or ask Zebulon if he had any questions. Zebulon just waved him to continue. Gaius talked about all of Sendal's industries, which were mining and forestry. He talked about the processing that each received before they were traded for what Sendal needed, like food stuff. There was a whole ten minutes on the companies who were controlled by the king and worked in those industries. Gaius talked about the mild weather and how that was good for the forestry. He talked about the princess's beauty and personality, without talking about her role in the politics of Sendal. He talked about the geography of the land and how that affected the main industries. On and on, he went.

Zebulon's eyes slowly closed on their own, even when Gaius tried to wake him up. Finally as Zebulon was close to falling asleep when there was a silence in the throne room that disturbed his sleep. Zebulon opened his eyes and saw Gaius had stopped talking to glare at him.

"Are you finished?" Zebulon asked around a yawn.

"No, Your Majesty," Gaius answered, "but I am not sure how there is going to be a treaty between our two kingdoms if you cannot listen to me explain what we have to offer."

"You have not said anything that I do not know already." Zebulon replied, "Proster has all the timber it needs from the forests that it is maintaining. We have enough mines to provide us with all the minerals we need. You have told us nothing about who your princess truly is, only that she sits on top of a glass pedestal to be admired but not interacted with. Less goes on in your kingdom than happens in Lithimin."

Gaius opened his mouth to retort.

"So, over all," Zebulon continued before Gaius could speak, "you have stood there and wasted my morning on a presentation that you have given multiple times in this court. Perhaps you would like to spend some time in your suite and come up with a new presentation that will not bore us to sleep."

"Yes, Your Majesty," Gaius replied before bowing. He turned and left the throne room.

"Dismissed," Zebulon said. Slowly everyone else left the throne room, except Herwin who stayed where he was standing behind Zebulon.

"If they are irritating you perhaps it is time to send them home," Herwin said.

"I told you that matter was closed to discussion," Zebulon replied.

"Have you thought about your wedding?" Herwin asked.

"I believe that for a wedding to take place there must be more than one person to stand at the altar," Zebulon said.

"It is the other party to whom I am asking about," Herwin said.

"Someone will come along," Zebulon said with an offhand wave.

"There have been several options presented to you," Herwin said.

"Do you mean the portraits?" Zebulon asked.

"They are good options," Herwin answered.

"I do not think this kingdom needs a queen from somewhere else." Zebulon said, "Any woman I marry will be from this kingdom and none other. I would rather marry for love than for a treaty."

"Have you any thoughts on which woman from Proster, you wish to marry?" Herwin asked.

"No," Zebulon relied, "I am sure that the answer will come to me one day."

"I would suggest sooner would be better than later," Herwin said.

"You cannot rush love." Zebulon said, "Love has its own schedule and its own way."

"As you wish," Herwin said with a bow. Herwin left the throne room, leaving Zebulon alone. Zebulon sat on his throne and waited several minutes. Then he went through his study to get to the staircase that led to the tower. He went up there and stood at the window. He watched without his spyglass for several minutes. The city looked the same as always. Zebulon took out his spyglass and searched the market place for the woman. He found her and her mother sitting in a stall in the market place. Her mother was leaning against her as if she was ill. They were not selling to anyone who had not bought from them before. No one else would come near them. They were going to have a lot of vegetables left and no money for food or medicine. No one was going to help them, or buy from them.

Zebulon put his spyglass away and headed back down the stairs. On the main floor, he stopped the first servant he saw.

"I need you to do a favour without telling anyone else I asked it of you," Zebulon told the servant.

"Yes, Sire," the servant said.

"I need you to go to the market." Zebulon said, "There is a stall with two women, one young and one old. The older one is sick. They are selling vegetables that they likely grew themselves."

"Yes, Sire," the servant said.

"Use this money to go and buy everything at that stall." Zebulon said as he took out a bag of coins and offered it to the servant, "Take the vegetables to the orphanage and give them to the cook."

"Yes, Sire," the servant said taking the bag.

"Thank you." Zebulon said, "If there is any money left you can keep it."

"Thank you, Sire," the servant bowed and then hurried away.

Zebulon went back up to the tower and took his spyglass out. He found the stall. They were still there. It looked like they could pack up, but the woman could not do it on her own. No one else was stopping at their stall, in fact everyone was hurrying passed to avoid them. Several minutes passed before Zebulon saw the servant arrive and buy all the vegetables. The servant put everything into a crate and took it all away. The women were happy about the money. They carefully left the stall with their belongings. The money would be enough for them to visit a healer and buy supper. Perhaps even feed them for a couple days.

This time Zebulon was happy as he closed the spyglass. They were taken care of for the moment and no one would connect it to him. It worked out well. He knew that he could not do it again anytime soon, because people could find out. That would be a bad thing.

Gaius was not willing to talk about the politics of Sendal and it was doubtful that he would ever be willing to do so. Zebulon had not outright asked anyone the political climate of their kingdom. All his information had come from inferring the situation based on what they had said. It did not mean he knew everything that was going on. He would have to find some other way to get the information he wanted about Sendal. Dard could get some of it because he could talk to the other people who had come with Gaius. Zebulon could not talk to those people without it looking suspicious. He was going to have to rely on Dard to get the information. Zebulon did not like that, but knew that Dard would be good for the information and trustable.

That left two more diplomats to learn the political situation of their kingdoms. Myles would be fairly easy. He was supposed to give a presentation the next time that court was held. If Zebulon was careful he could ask questions without Myles knowing what he wanted. Myles was always willing to give information if it meant he could talk about the five portraits he brought with him. Zebulon was willing to listen this time.

Zebulon headed back down the stairs. He reached the bottom as a servant was coming down the hallway.

"Lunch is ready, Sire," the servant said with a bow.

"Thank you," Zebulon said before heading to the dining room.

After lunch, Zebulon allowed the cases that could not be settled in the lower court to be heard in his court. He spent the afternoon listening to people bringing their problems to him. He solved them the best he could. It took all his energy and all afternoon before the cases had all been heard. Zebulon refused the break Herwin offered, in the middle of the afternoon because he knew that it would prevent them from getting through everything.

Once all the cases had been heard and decided upon the court was dismissed again. Everyone left the throne room, except Zebulon. He sat there for half an hour with only his thoughts. He was just about to get to his feet when the servant he asked to help the women entered the throne room.

"Yes?" Zebulon asked.

"I did as you asked." the servant replied, "The orphanage was happy to receive the vegetables. They had lacked over the last few days as no one has had extra that they were willing to donate. I also donated the rest of the money you gave me. I had no need for it and they still lacked. I told them neither my name, nor the name of the person who sent me, but they said to pass on their thanks."

"Thank you," Zebulon said.

"You are welcome, Sire," the servant said before bowing and leaving the throne room.

Zebulon smiled as he sat there for a few moments longer. Then he stood up and left the throne room. Rather than head toward the dining room and supper, Zebulon went up to his bed chamber. He checked it over before locking and barring the door behind him. Zebulon then crawled into bed and let the tiredness take him.

Zebulon rolled over and looked around. The sky outside his window was purple. He still felt tired, but something had woken him up. He laid there and listened. His senses told him that there was no one in his room. The door was still barred. The scratching sound came again. Zebulon could not identify where it came from. There was a long pause before it came again. It was not coming from anywhere inside the room. Zebulon got out of bed making as little sound as possible. He was still wearing his clothes from yesterday, so did not have to find any as he carefully walked around the room listening for the scratching sound. He had to wait through the pauses for the sound to come again.

He tried the inside walls first, but the sound was not coming from the hallway. He went to each side wall, but it was not coming from the rooms on either side of his. Finally he went to the wall on the outside. This time the scratching was loudest. The sound was coming from outside. It hardly seemed possible that anyone could get up to his window. The window itself was hardly big enough for a person to get through it, if that person could get up the wall. However, it was the back wall of the castle, so no one would notice a person climbing up.

Zebulon opened his window. It opened inward, so the person could not see if it was open or not. Zebulon crept to the window and looked out. There was a figure clad in black clothing with only the area around his eyes visible climbing up the wall toward the window. The man was likely thin enough to fit through the window. The scratching sound was his climbing gear, which seemed to be able to hold him without obvious signs of support. It was strange, but so was the way the man moved. It was almost like the way a spider moved.

The man looked up and his purple eyes met Zebulon's eyes. They stared at each other for several minutes. Those eyes looked closer to elven than human, but elven eyes would be more slanted in the face. The man had stopped climbing and just hung there staring up at Zebulon. Zebulon was sure that the man was more than able to kill him and yet he did not feel any fear.

A wolf howled in the distance. It was loud and carried a warning with it. The man looked toward the trees that grew behind the castle as if he understood the howling. Then he looked back at Zebulon. Their eyes met and the man nodded. Then the man broke eye contact to start climbing back down. The white wolf came to Zebulon's mind. The howling had stopped, but the man kept doing down the wall. Zebulon stood there and watched until the man was out of sight. Then Zebulon pulled his head in and closed the window.

Zebulon changed clothes before going down to his study. Reaching it he checked it over carefully for traps before sitting down in the chair. There was no paperwork for him to do and no books he wanted to read. He took out a book of blank paper. His father had the book made along several other volumes to write down the history.

All but this volume had been filled. Zebulon had not bothered to write down the history. He had funded others to do such things, but now he had an interest in this blank volume. Zebulon opened it to the first page and dipped his quill in the ink. With care he drew the image of the white wolf on the paper. Under it he listed all that he knew of the wolf. It was a short list.

When he was finished with the wolf, Zebulon turned the page and started drawing a picture of the man who had been climbing to his window. Under that image, he wrote everything he knew of the man. Again this was not much. With this information down, he took out a book on magical beings that had been one of his father's prized possessions. His father had several books on magical things. These were creatures that were magical. He flipped through it looking for pictures that matched the one he had drawn.

He found a wolf, but it was different and much more menacing. However, half way through the book he found the man. The man was called a Reeze. There was only one in the whole world and it was immortal. It lived through eating the souls of beings that it killed. It hired itself out as an assassin, but money was worthless to it, so other methods of payment had to be found. There was very little that the Reeze feared and few agreements it kept.

Zebulon wondered why the Reeze had stopped for climbing the rest of the way and killing him. Was it the wolf? If so, what was between the wolf and the Reeze? The wolf had done nothing but protect him so far, but Zebulon did not know why. None of it made much sense. Zebulon as thankful for it anyway. Zebulon closed both books and put them back on the shelf.

Magic had all but disappeared since his father's time. There used to be demons to fight and magical objects around. Since the demon that took the children, there had not been any to fight. Wizards and witches were also not around to cause trouble. Something had caused the magic to disappear. Zebulon did not know what it was, but it was a good thing. He knew that he had no ability to defend the kingdom against magical beings. His father's sword, the Wizard Slayer, had disappeared with Narda. Since it had not been needed, Zebulon had accepted that it was now Narda's sword. He had been given a very decorative sword when he became king, but he used one of his father's practical ones if he needed to use one. It worked best.

Zebulon went to the dining room. He was served breakfast and left alone to eat. There were very few people awake and eating at this time of the morning. Of those that were up, very little conversation was heard.

After breakfast, Zebulon went up to the tower, but a search of the market place showed no sign of the woman. She was probably with her mother. He could understand if they were not there today. He missed seeing her and could feel the hallow space in his heart that came when he did not see her. He longed to go and find her, but knew he could not do that.

Zebulon shook himself out of it as he took the spyglass from his eye. He closed it and put it away. There was no use to stay up here and wishing for things that were not going to happen. He headed back down the stairs. He might as well hold court again. At the bottom of the stairs, he headed for the throne room. It was empty as it was supposed to be. Zebulon went to his throne, but did not sit down. Something made him walk around the throne first. In the back of it he found the trap that would have imbedded the poisoned knife into his back. He carefully disarmed it and got rid of the knife.

When he got back to the throne room, Zebulon found the Reeze sitting on his throne. The Reeze was still clad in all black with only his eyes visible. He had one leg over the arm of the throne and an arm hanging on the back of it.

"Are you here to kill me?" Zebulon asked as he stopped just short of the dais.

"No," the Reeze answered, "the contract was offered, but I have to refuse to fulfill it. You are lucky in your allies."

"The wolf?" Zebulon asked.

"You know nothing of her?" the Reeze asked, "Perhaps she is not ready to tell you. As she is your ally, I will not kill you, but you should know that you have discontent within your kingdom."

"I am aware." Zebulon said, "It is not the first time, nor likely to be the last. Would you be willing to tell me which one made the contract?"

"He did not tell me who he was." the Reeze said, "He wore a black cloak to our meeting and I could not see his face. He knew the spell to summon me, but had no magical ability. It is unlikely that he will use magic again to attack you. There is very little left here."

"That is good to know," Zebulon said.

"I fear it is the little good news you will hear in a long while," the Reeze said, "but I have been told that I should not tell you anymore. I can tell you that you will see the white wolf again. She unlikely to tell you anything, but you will see her again. Me, however, you will never see again."

Zebulon nodded. The Reeze disappeared without so much as a puff of smoke, or a flash of light. Zebulon checked the throne before sitting down in it. He had just made himself comfortable, when he remembered the would-be assassin attached to the table in the dungeon. Zebulon got up and headed down to the dungeon. He had not met anyone in the hallways except the occasional servant. The rest of the people likely would not be up for another hour or so.

Zebulon reached the dungeon and went in the door. He walked passed the cells to the second room. The would-be assassin was lying there on the table. There was blood at his wrist and ankles where he had tried to escape, but had not succeeded. His eyes held a worried look, but he kept it from the rest of his face.

"You were supposed to kill me," Zebulon said. The man stared up at the ceiling and did not answer.

"You failed," Zebulon said, "and I am willing to give you a pardon if you tell me who hired you."

The man glanced at Zebulon for only a brief moment before going back to staring at the ceiling.

"If you do not tell me what I want to know, I cannot guarantee anything," Zebulon said, "and I have a man among my court who loves to inflict pain on people. I will charge him with getting the information out of you and it is unlikely he will leave you in any condition that you can leave this place."

The man did not move, but fear was in his eyes as his thoughts brought up the images of pain. Zebulon went over to the tool bench. The metal items that littered it were likely too rusty to be used and Zebulon had no idea what any of them were for. They all looked nasty. Zebulon studied them as if he had an interest in them.

"The tools of torture are so fascinating, do you not think?" Zebulon asked, "I once thought I wanted to know how to do it, but my first lesson was unfortunately my last. My stomach is not of the right strength to deal with it, even if my head thinks so. Have you known the glory of torture?" Zebulon did not look up at the man, but saw him out of the corner of his eye.

The man had gone pale and was trying not to squirm on the table. He was scared, but was not ready to admit it.

"Sometimes the best place to be during torture sessions is on a bench in the other room," Zebulon said, "where the screaming is so close and so loud. The dungeon walls are too thick to hear it anywhere else, which is such a pity. It is so exciting when you are in court and the sound of pain comes up through the floor. People look at each other and give in to me. It gives me almost god like abilities. And my torturer can keep people screaming for weeks. He is one of the best at causing pain in the world. He likes living here because I do not put any limits on what he can do. As long as he keeps the screams going for as long as possible, he can do anything he wants."

The man was trying to swallow with his dry throat. He was struggling against his bonds.

"Now," Zebulon came back over to the table, "will you give up who hired you in exchange for a pardon, or do I have to find my torturer?"

"Pardon," the man gasped out.

"Wonderful choice," Zebulon said before getting the man a glass of water. He gave the man a drink.

"Now, who hired you?" Zebulon asked when the man had finished.

"Atius, the Lithimin diplomat, and a man wearing a black cloak." the man answered, "I did not see the face of the second man, but he was taller than Atius. I took the job because I needed the money for my family."

"Thank you," Zebulon said, "I will be back in a moment."

Zebulon left the dungeon. He found the steward pacing back and forth just inside the doorway of the throne room.

"Your Majesty," the steward said when he saw Zebulon, "I need to speak with you."

"Go ahead," Zebulon said.

"The assistant to Gaius was found dead outside the kitchen door." the steward said, "He has no injuries and there is no apparent cause of death. Just me and the head cook know about this; I have not told anyone else. What should be done?"

"Have Gaius come to me." Zebulon said, "Once you have done that, take a guard and a pouch of money down to the dungeon. There you will release the man we put in there the other evening. The guard is to take him to the border of Menano and leave him there with the money."

"Yes, Your Majesty," the steward said with a bow. He left the throne room.

Zebulon did not sit down on the throne, but on the edge of the dais. He waited there several minutes before Gaius and Myles arrived.

"I wish to speak to Gaius alone," Zebulon said.

"As you wish, Your Majesty," Myles bowed and left the throne room.

"What is it that you want to speak with me about?" Gaius asked.

"Your assistant has been found dead this morning." Zebulon answered, "It is believed that he was poisoned. I do not know who did it or why, but it was not on anyone's order that I am aware of. I will start an investigation about the whole thing."

"That is very generous of you," Gaius said, "but I think it would be best if I take his body home."

"It was not an offer." Zebulon said, "As such, his body will be taken home by an undertaker from the city. You will remain here until the investigation has reached its conclusion."

"You cannot keep me here against me will," Gaius said.

"I do not wish to do so, but I want this death investigated." Zebulon said, "A greater war may be prevented by the outcome of the investigation, even if a minor quarrel comes before it. I want everyone to know who is responsible for the death, so that there is no question of who is to blame."

"As you wish, Your Majesty." Gaius said, "My people will cooperate."

"Good," Zebulon said.

Gaius bowed and left the throne room. Zebulon stood up and started to pace the floor in front of the dais. It was the area his father used to walk when he was dealing with a vexing problem. Zebulon noted this and kept pacing. He had a death to have investigated, three people grouped together to kill him, and treaties to negotiate. He needed to learn the political environment of the kingdoms who wanted treaties with him.

The steward entered the throne room causing Zebulon to stop pacing and look at him.

"The guard and the man are off," the steward said.

"Good," Zebulon said, "I told Gaius about the death of his assistant. I also told him that body would be sent back with an undertaker from the city and an investigation into the death. No one is to leave the city until the investigation is completed."

"Shall I inform Herwin about the investigation?" the steward asked.

"Is Garrick in the city, or has he returned to his estate?" Zebulon asked.

"He is in the city," the steward said.

"Then ask him to do the investigation," Zebulon replied.

"Is there anything further?" the steward asked.

"Not at the moment," Zebulon answered.

"Then I will go do as asked," the steward bowed to Zebulon before leaving the throne room.

Zebulon went to the throne and sat down. The rest of the court would arrive within the hour and then Myles would give his presentation. Zebulon had lots to think about before then.

THE LAST TALK OF POLITICS, A DECISION, AND CONSEQUENCES

Zebulon showed more interest as Myles gave his presentation about the portraits he brought with him. He talked about the women, one at a time and in full detail. Based on what Myles said about their role in the kingdom, Zebulon gleaned a few things about the political environment of the kingdom. The first being that the population was three females for every one male. The main industries were farming and mining, with enough forests to satisfy their need for lumber. They traded with their neighbours, of which Proster was not one, for anything that they could not get for themselves. All those trade agreements were solid and enjoyed by both sides. The king kept the citizens happy as possible, but lacked in sons. He had plenty of daughters that he was willing to marry off to anyone of high enough rank that asked. If Zebulon was not single, Myles would not have been sent there at all. The biggest problem in the kingdom was the ratio of men to women and no one had any idea what to do about it, except to look for places that were in need of women.

Even if Zebulon had not discounted Myles on the basis that he was shorter than Atius, the presentation certainly did. Myles was not worried about politics, or trading. He gained nothing from Zebulon being removed from the throne. He gained nothing from any of this, except if Zebulon chose to marry one of the portraits. That did not mean he was bored and ready to head back, but when the time came he would leave without a backward glance.

When Myles was finished his presentation, the court went to the dining room for lunch. Court was over for the day. Zebulon finished eating before leaving the dining room. He went up to the tower. Taking out the spyglass, Zebulon searched the market place for the woman. He found her and her mother at a stall trying to sell their vegetables. She was calling out to the people passing by while her mother was sitting at the back of the stall. She looked to be recovering from her illness, which was good. People were not going passed in a hurry, but they did not buy anything either. The only people who stopped were the regular customers. Zebulon wondered whether they actually needed the vegetables or they bought things out of pity for the woman and her mother.

The sound of footsteps could be heard coming up the stairs. Zebulon listened for a moment before relaxing. The person was doing nothing to be quiet. When the footsteps got closer, Zebulon closed the spyglass and put it away. Finally Dard stumbled up the final steps and collapsed against the wall under the window. Zebulon took out the spyglass and went back to watching the woman.

"Gaius has his people on tight strings." Dard said once he had caught his breath, "It is very hard to find one who would talk."

"You got his assistant to talk," Zebulon said.

"How did you know?" Dard asked.

"Gaius's assistant was found dead this morning," Zebulon answered.

"What are you doing about it?" Dard asked.

"Garrick is going to investigate it and report his findings." Zebulon answered, "Do any of Gaius's people connect you to looking for information for me?"

"I do not believe so." Dard answered, "I was not directly involved in asking then for the information."

"That is good." Zebulon said, "What did you find out?"

"Sendal is a troubled kingdom." Dard answered, "The king is a tyrant, but he has to be. Sendal is short on food and he has to protect and ration what little there is. It needs to gain food through trade because it cannot afford to buy it. Likely they are trading favours for food."

"I talked to two would be assassins," Zebulon said, "and both describe a man in a black cloak hiring them. The one said that the cloaked man was taller than Atius."

"Of the five only Myles and Jarlan are shorter than Atius," Dard said, "that leaves Gaius or Luce as our third conspirator. Luce only brought one servant and I have not been able to find a way to that person. I have been trying to keep an eye on Luce, but he seems to wander the castle as he pleases. I think he uses magic as well."

"Why would you think that?" Zebulon asked.

"Little things," Dard answered, "the lightning if a person gets too close to the door of his rooms, the powder he sprinkles on his food, and the strangeness of his one servant. It all resembles magic to me."

"So, we really do not know anything about Wodend and its political environment," Zebulon said, "but we know that Gaius would join in if there was food promised to his people. We need to find out which of the two is the third conspirator."

"I have not found any agreements between Gaius and the other two." Dard said, "I have seen Luce talking to Jarlan a few times. The last discussion I saw looked intense. I do not know what they were talking about, but there was something going on."

"Something will come up," Zebulon said, "especially if we are both looking for information."

"I hope so," Dard said.

Zebulon turned his attention back to the woman. She was working hard at getting people interested, but they still were not buying. Zebulon remembered her voice from the day riding passed. The way it made him want to see her. The feeling of warmth in his chest. The joy of first seeing her; of knowing that she was the one woman for him. The emptiness when he looked for her and she was not there. She was the only thing missing from his life. Without her, he was nothing. His crown was meaningless, his life was purposeless, and his kingdom might as well belong to Grackle. Everything that was currently wrong made him want to be in her arms because there everything would be all right.

But she did not know any of this. She was just trying to survive. It was not likely that she was sitting there dreaming about him. She might even turn him down. He could not blame her if she did. While she was down there starving, he was up here comfortable while he watched her. It had been two years since he first saw her in the market place and not once during that time did he find the nerve to talk to her. The feelings inside him merely got pressed down and now they all wanted to bubble to the surface. He knew he had press them down again at least until the current situation had resolved itself.

"Why do you not just go down and talk to her?" Dard asked, "You do not even have to tell her everything, you just have to say hello and ask her name."

"I am not ready yet," Zebulon answered, "I will be after this problem with the diplomats is over."

"And what about the problem after that?" Dard asked as he got to his feet, "And the one after that? Do you have to wait for them all?" Dard turned to look out the window. "Part of the problem with the diplomats will not be over under you announce your engagement. You cannot do that until you have asked her to marry you. I am sure that Herwin has gotten on your case recently to pick someone to marry. If you go down and say hello, you have gone the first steps toward where you want to be. Everyone else is busy today, so there will not be anyone following you down to the market place. No one will know you have a woman you are interested in. All you have to do is go down there and say hello. Ask her what her name is. It is easy. She runs a stall, you can be interested in the vegetables to start things off. As long as you buy some and take it with you, she will not think you went down there to meet her."

Zebulon felt almost hypnotized by Dard's words. It sounded so simple. Just go down there and ask the woman what her name was. It would be a beginning and he would learn a lot from it. If she brushed him off, then he knew she was not interested in him. He was not sure what to do if she was not interested in him, but he would deal with that when he got there. All he had to do was go down there.

With everything that was happening at the castle, no one would miss him if he disappeared for an hour or two. He would not be around for the afternoon either way. The different would be that he was in the market instead of up here. And he could go say hello without taking her back to the castle to be put into a situation that no one deserved to be in the centre of. He would take money with him and pretend to be interested in the vegetables. It would be easy.

"Fine," Zebulon said as he closed his spyglass and put it away.

"Great," Dard said, "let us find you something to wear, so that you do not stand out."

"I think I have some clothes in my wardrobe," Zebulon said as he started down the stairs. Dard followed him.

When they reached the bottom, they were careful as they made their way to Zebulon's bed chamber. They avoided being seen. In the bed chamber, Zebulon went to the wardrobe and rummaged through it until he found the bundle of clothing that he was looking for. He pulled it out and unrolled it. There was a shirt and trousers with a pair of shoes. All there dirty, rumbled, and worn. Dard looked them over critically, then looked over Zebulon.

"Do they still fit?" Dard asked.

"I do not know," Zebulon answered, "I have not worn them in years." Zebulon took the clothed behind the screen and changed into them. He came out to show Dard. The trousers were an inch too short and the sleeves on the shirt kept riding up.

"The shoes still fit," Zebulon pointed out.

"I will be right back with clothes that will work," Dard said. He left Zebulon's bed chamber. Zebulon changed back to his regular clothes. He wrapped the clothes back up, without the shoes, and tossed them on the chair in the corner. A servant would take them and likely turn them into rags. Zebulon sat down with the book he had left in the room while he waited for Dard.

Dard arrived back less than ten minutes later. He was carrying a bundle under one arm.

"Here you go," Dard offered it to Zebulon.

"Thank you," Zebulon put down the book and accepted the bundle. He took it behind the screen and changed into these clothes. This time when he came back out, he looked much more like a peasant than a boy with a recent growth spurt.

"Looks good enough for me," Dard said.

"Good," Zebulon said, "you stay at the castle and see what you can find out and I will go down to the market."

"As you wish," Dard said. He bowed and then left the room. Zebulon gathered everything else he would need to go to the market place, like a pouch of coins and a cloak. When he was ready he took a deep breath and left his bed chamber. He moved through the halls of the castle avoiding people until he came to the door to the court yard that he wanted. He left the castle and went across the court yard. No one paid any attention to him. Lots of people go across this court yard every day and they all have some reason for it. And since he was leaving he was not considered a problem. He walked through the gates undisturbed.

Zebulon headed down the streets to the market place. It was not that far, but some of the streets caused him confusion because he had not been to the market place in a while. And last time had been by carriage. However, if he ever got too far turned around, Zebulon would just listen for the sounds of the market place and that would get him going in the right direction. The sounds had led him down one street, but he found that it was a dead end. He was about to turn back when Zebulon saw an alley way. He went down it and found the sound of the market place was louder here. Zebulon was just about to the end of the alley way when he picked up one voice from the rest. It was the woman.

Zebulon stopped in the alley way where he could see her. She was still trying to get people to buy her vegetables by going into the street toward them. She still was not getting very many sales. Zebulon watched her. Her black hair and blue eyes made it easy to follow her as she moved around. He wanted to go over there and say hello, but he did not move. He wanted to go over there and ask her what her name was, but he did not move. The voice of Dard became a nag in his head, insisting that he go over there and talk to her. The arguments for talking to her came into his head. The shame that would come from going back to the castle without having talked to her was there as well. Zebulon did not move from the alley way. He wanted to, but he was stuck in quicksand and it would not loosen its hold long enough for him to move. He wanted her to be with him and to love him. He wanted her to just tell him her name. He wanted to tell her his without it being a royal decree. Somehow he could not move to do any of these things. He struggled, but it was useless.

Zebulon did not want to turn away either, so he stood there and watched her. From this distance he could see more of her and the things she dealt with to run her stall. The other people who were around. The poor people who went passed that would have bought something if they had money. The ones with a little money who had bought food from other stalls. The richer ones who walked by with their noses in the air as if they could not stand breathing the same air as her. Most of the people who bought from her were the ones that fit in the middle of rich and poor. They had money to afford food, but very little else. Their clothes were not the best and they were as dirty as the rest of the people walking the streets. Zebulon was surprised by the number of poor who walked passed without money to buy anything. He was always told that everyone had enough and that Proster was a rich kingdom. About one in ten people that went passed looked rich, but only five of the nine who were left had money for food. That left five in every ten who were poor and needed food. That was a sad statistic.

Zebulon had watched the woman for so long, he wondered why he had never noticed this. But then the people moved around and he could see her again. The rest of the world seemed to melt away. She was the working poor. She had no money, but survived because she could grow some vegetables to sell to other people. She looked like she could help him get to know the true population of his kingdom. She would know how people felt. The people he did not come in contact with because he was removed from them by the people who had declared themselves his protectors, Herwin and Garrick and other members of the court. His father had always been able to know what the people needed, but Zebulon never figure out how he did it. So, he never figured out how to do it. Perhaps he needed to spend some time in the lower court to hear the people and their problems. He could spend more time in the market place talking with the people there. He could beg the woman to marry him so that she could teach him what it was like.

He came down here to say hello and ask her what her name was. Instead he was standing in an alley way unable take five steps out and say anything. It was not that hard to do. He even had the excuse of looking to buy vegetables. The money was in his coin pouch. He could just go over there and say he wanted to buy some vegetables. It would be easy as soon as he got his legs to move.

There was a scream from down the street, but no one looked up or paid attention. It was too far away. Zebulon noted it, but ignored it as he watched the woman. Then there was the sound of wheels on cobblestones headed in this direction. Zebulon looked up to see the carriage barreling down the street. It was black and red with the crest of Lord Breton's family. The carriage was going much too fast for traveling along that street. People heard the carriage, looked up, and ran out of its way, usually getting to safety just in time. Zebulon lost sight of the woman as the carriage went passed the alley way, but she had been running to get out of the way along with everyone else. Zebulon saw Angus riding in the back, laughing with Orestes about something. Then they were gone and the carriage was disappearing down the street.

The scream of horror and despair came from the street in front of the alley way. Zebulon took his eyes from where the carriage went and moved to the mother of the woman who was rushing out of the stall to the figure on the ground. The woman had been hit by the carriage and was now lying on the street. Her mother reached her and wrapped the woman in her arms. The mother was sobbing. From this distance, the woman gave no signs of life. Fear gripped Zebulon's heart as he watched everyone else moved away from the scene. The mother just sat there in the middle of the street holding her daughter and crying. Zebulon wanted to go and help her, but he could not move. He felt like someone else had taken over his body and he was getting to watch.

The six guards arrived and talked to people around to get the story. They checked on the woman, but the shaking of the head told Zebulon that she was gone. There was no question about it. Two of the guards helped the mother pack up her stall and then escorted her home. It was difficult for them because she did not want to leave her daughter and she could not afford the services of an undertaker. They finally got her away from there. One guard was left to watch over the body until the undertaker arrived while the rest moved on up the street to see what other damage was done by the carriage.

Zebulon still had not moved. Someone had scooped out everything inside him and left a hollow shell. His mind was empty, his heart was empty, and all that was left was an icy coldness. His life was worthless, this kingdom was kingless, and his world had disappeared into a lightless tunnel. It might as well be him lying there unmoving in the street.

The undertaker arrived in his wagon. He stopped and got down. The guard helped him put the body on the back of the wagon. Then the guard headed up the street. The undertaker got up into the driver's seat of the wagon and got his horses moving.

Without realizing what he was doing, Zebulon left the alley way and followed the undertaker's wagon. He followed it to the mortuary. The undertaker took the wagon around back, but Zebulon went in the front door. There was a woman sitting on a stool in a room full of coffins. There was another door that must have gone to the back. The woman was likely the undertaker's wife.

"Can I help?" the undertaker's wife asked.

"Yes," Zebulon answered as he took out the pouch of coins, "use this to pay for the burial of the woman the undertaker just brought in. And if there is any left give it to the woman's mother."

"Certainly," the undertaker's wife said taking the offered pouch. Her eyes widened as she felt the weight.

Zebulon turned to leave.

"Is there a name I can give her along with the money?" the undertaker's wife asked.

"No," Zebulon said and then left.

The afternoon was bright and sunny, but Zebulon saw the world as dark. He did not head back to the castle. There was nothing there worth going back for. Instead he just started to wander in the opposite direction.

Night fell without Zebulon really noticing. He had wandered into the poor part of the city, which was closest to the wall. No one paid him any attention. He was just another lost soul in the city. There were plenty in this part of the city. Most stayed close to the buildings and alley way. Some had obvious losses like limbs, but others the only sign of their loss was the look in their eyes. Zebulon was not aware of any of these people. As the lamps were lit by the guards that patrolled the area, the people would move into whatever shelter they had, whether it is an old building or an alley way. Zebulon could not feel his feet getting tired or his stomach rumble, the only thing he was aware of was the emptiness in his chest.

As the night rolled on, he wandered through more streets without any idea of distance or direction. Some places were darker than others. In some places eyes peered out of the darkness, but no one moved as Zebulon stumbled passed. There was no reason to stop him. He had no food and did not look like he had any money. His cloak might be a little more expensive, but the clothes underneath were rags just as everyone else had.

The sun rose and lit up the streets. The guards put out the lamps as they went passed them on their patrol. The buildings were in need of replacing, but some people tried to keep their houses in good repair. There were a few that were rubble and still people lived there. Zebulon was starting to go back along streets he had been down before. This time no one even glanced up at him. The people left him alone and the guards did not bother with him. He was left to his own thoughts, which were empty of all but one thing.

There were more people out once the sun was at its height in the sky. The smells of food drifted along the breeze. Those that had food bought lunch home to feed their family. Those without food were in the market place begging for what they could get. Zebulon's stomach might have growled and rumbled with hunger, but he did not notice. He just put one foot in front of the other with any attention to his surroundings.

Zebulon was not sure how long he had been wandering, but he found himself standing in front of a fountain that no longer had water in it. Instead there was an older man in rags sitting on the edge. Night had fallen and the only light came from street lamps. Zebulon's stomach rumbled, but he did not want to find food. His feet hurt, but he did not care. There was nothing in the world he wanted but to lose himself again. He had come to the market place hoping to gain a sense of wholeness, instead he lost everything that gave his life meaning.

Zebulon's knees gave out and he sat down on the edge of the fountain. If there had been a cliff nearby, he might have dropped himself off it.

"It is not all lost," the voice of the old man interrupted Zebulon's thoughts.

"You do not even know what is wrong." Zebulon said, "How could you possibly know whether it is all lost or not?"

"I have seen that look on many a man." the old man said, "You lost your love. Life goes on after love, this is not the end. You can move beyond this, you just have to find something else to live for."

"Without love, what else in life is there to live for?" Zebulon asked.

"I cannot tell you that," the old man answered, "every person has to find their own meaning and purpose. If I tried to tell you what yours was it likely would not be true. Only you can find the meaning and purpose for your life. But you must search your soul for what that is."

"And how does a person do that?" Zebulon asked.

"Perhaps a story will help you understand," the old man answered.

"I will listen," Zebulon said, "but I do not expect it to help."

THE PRINCE AND HIS SEARCH FOR MEANING

The prince rode deep into the haunted forest. He suppressed the fear in his heart and rode on. His love was in the centre of the forest and he had to rescue her.

The path appeared and he went along it because it was faster than riding through the bush. He rode along it for a ways then he saw a woman just off the path. He reined in his horse and stopped beside the woman. She was old by her looks and ugly by her features.

"How far am I from the centre of the forest?" the prince demanded.

"A distance that is long and short," the old woman replied, "Your heart determines the distance you must ride."

"Am I headed in the correct direction?" the prince asked.

"The heart knows the way," the old woman replied.

"If I knew the way, I would not have to stop and ask you," the prince said.

"Would you help a poor woman?" the old woman asked in a creaky voice.

"It depends on what help is needed," the prince said.

"I lost my dog," the old woman said, "He ran off after a deer and he has not come back. I am worried about him, but I cannot walk that far."

"I will see if I can track your dog," the prince said as he got down from his horse. He tied the reins to a nearby tree.

"Which way did it go?" the prince asked.

"That way," the old woman pointed into the bush.

The prince headed in the direction the woman pointed. It was difficult going through the bush and around trees, but he had found the dog's paw prints in the moist ground. He followed them through some heavy bush deeper into this part of the forest. It got harder to go through and several times he was not sure he could get through, but the prince kept going. The prince noticed that the ground was rising. It was a gradual rise at first, but got steeper fairly quickly. It got to the point where the prince was grabbing branches to pull himself up. The paw prints showed that the dog also had problems here, but the dog had continued on, so did the prince. The prince reached the top of the hill, but there were too many trees to see anything from there. He followed the paw prints down the hill that was steep at first and then was not as bad. When the slope disappeared again the brush become thick and trees grew closer together. The prince found that branches pulled at his clothes as he pressed through. It was hard work, but he followed the paw prints that he could find.

The prince came upon a clearing and entered it. He found the dog trapped in brambles on the other side. The deer was nowhere in sight.

"Silly dog," the prince said with a smile as he kneeled down to pet the dog's nose. The dog whined. The prince took out his knife and carefully extracted the dog from the brambles. The dog happily licked the prince's face.

"Let us get you back to your owner," the prince said. The dog barked a yes and they headed back to the path the prince had made getting there. They went through the brush. The dog followed the prince because the brush was thick and he had difficult time getting through it. They reached the hill, both struggled up it and then down the other side. They walked the long way back, through some thick bush and around trees.

Finally they reached the place where the old woman was waiting. She greeted the dog with a smile and the dog greeted her by licking her face.

"Thank you," the old woman said to the prince.

"You are welcome," the prince said as he got back up on his horse. He continued along the path.

He rode for several hours as he tried to get to the centre of the forest and his love. It was impossible to tell what time a day it was. It was light, but the sun and sky could not be seen through the tree branches. The prince stopped for nothing because he was determined to reach his love and rescue her.

He came across a girl, who was standing on the side of the path. The prince reined in his horse and stopped by the girl. The girl was wearing a green dress and was perhaps fourteen in age.

"How far am I from the centre of the forest?" the prince demanded.

"*A distance that is long and short,*" the girl replied, "*Your heart determines the distance you must ride.*"

"*Am I headed in the correct direction?*" the prince asked.

"*The heart knows the way,*" the girl replied.

"*If I knew the way, I would not have to stop and ask you,*" the prince said.

"*Would you help a poor girl?*" the girl asked in a high voice.

"*It depends on what help is needed,*" the prince said.

"*My mother's necklace was stolen by an ogre that lives in a cave,*" the girl said, "*Can you get it back for me?*"

"*I can try,*" the prince said as he got down off his horse and tied the reins to a tree, "*Which way is the cave of this ogre?*"

"*That way,*" the girl pointed into the forest.

The prince went in the direction the girl had pointed. The brush was thick, but it was easy to get through along paths that the ogre must have left. He walked along for a ways before he came on definite traces of the ogre. He followed them to a hilly area and a cave opening. The prince drew his sword when he arrived at the cave.

"*A girl claims you stole her necklace,*" the prince called into the cave, "*I am here to get it back for her.*"

"*If you want it, you have to fight me for it,*" the ogre called back.

There was a light coming from deep in the cave and around a bend. The prince was careful as he entered the cave and went deep into it. He eyes slowly adjusted to the darkness as he made his way deeper into the cave. He came to the bend in the tunnel. The prince went around it and found the ogre standing there waiting beside a fire.

The ogre had a club in his hand. He gave a war cry as he charged at the prince. The prince stood there until just before the ogre reached him and then stepped to one side and let the ogre continued passed. The ogre stopped his charge and turned to the prince. The ogre used his club and the prince used his sword as they battled in the light of the fire.

Ability and stamina won out and the ogre ended up run through with the prince's sword. The prince wiped off his sword and then searched the cave for the necklace. He found it in one corner. The prince took it and left the cave. He walked back through the trails in the bush.

Finally the prince arrived back to the place where the girl was waiting. He handed her the necklace. The girl happily took it.

"Thank you," the girl said.

"You are welcome," the prince said as he got back up on his horse. He continued along the path.

He rode on. He doubted at moments that this path would take him to the centre of the forest, but he did not want to ride through the bush. The prince came upon a pool of water. He stopped and rested. He ate while his horse drank. When he was rested, the prince got back on his horse and continued on. His love was in the centre of the forest and he had to get there to rescue her.

The prince came around the bend in the path and saw a man on the side of the path. The man had a long white beard, ragged clothing, and tears in his eyes. The prince reined in his horse and stopped near the sad man.

"How far am I from the centre of the forest?" the prince demanded.

"A distance that is long and short," the sad man replied, "Your heart determines the distance you must ride."

"Am I headed in the correct direction?" the prince asked.

"The heart knows the way," the sad man replied.

"If I knew the way, I would not have to stop and ask you," the prince said.

"Would you help a poor man?" the sad man asked in a rough voice.

"It depends on what help is needed," the prince said.

"My wife was kidnapped by a band of thieves," the sad man said, "They dragged her off with the threat that they would kill her if I did not get money for them."

"I will see if I can find your wife and save her," the prince said as he got down from his horse. He tied the reins to a nearby tree.

"Which way did the thieves go?" the prince asked.

"That way," the sad man pointed into the bush.

The prince headed in the direction to the sad man pointed. The brush was thick for the first while, but soon there trees grew farther apart and the underbrush was not as bad. This let the prince see the tracks of the band of thieves. He followed them.

The tracks wandered all over the place as if they were worried about going in a straight line. Every once in a while they seemed to stop before going off in a different direction. They went up some hills that they could have gone around and down into valley to jump over creeks. There were twelve individual sets of prints, plus the drag marks of a thirteenth person.

It got dark and with the tree branches overhead it was difficult to see. The prince slowed down and was careful as he continued forward. A yellow light appeared in the distance. The prince went toward the light and found the ground start to slope downward. He reached a ledge where the slope dropped sharply and crawled out on to it so that he could look over it. In the valley below the prince could see the thieves' camp. The light came from their bonfire. The prince crawled back off the ledge. He made his way towards the camp. The light from the fire was enough to see where he was going.

As the prince got closer, he crouched down and kept behind bushes to avoid being seen by the thieves. When he finally reached the bushes just outside the camp, he stopped behind a bush to see what was going on. The thieves were sitting around the fire eating something that smelled like chicken. There were some barrels to one side of the camp along with crates of supplies. The sad man's wife was tied to a tree and appeared to be unharmed.

One of the thieves got up and went over to the barrels. He poured something into a jug from the tap on the barrel. He set the jug on top of the barrel before looking for something. He did not find it so he wandered back to where he had been sitting and continued to look. The prince snuck around the outside of the camp to where the barrels were. He took out a small bottle with a sleeping potion in it. The prince moved carefully to avoid being seen and poured the potion into the jug. Then he moved back and hid in the bushes again. The thief came back for the jug. He poured a cup before passing it to the next thief. It went around the circle of thieves and then was set back on the barrel.

The prince waited as he watched the thieves drink what was in their cups and then refill them with again. As they finished their second cups, they started to fall asleep. The prince waited until they were all snoring. He left his hiding place and went over to the sad man's wife. She looked up at him. He put his finger to his lips. She nodded. He cut the ropes holding her. When she was free, he grabbed a stick to use as a torch and they left the thieves and their fire behind. They went back up the slope and though the forest.

Finally they arrived back at where the sad man was waiting. The man and his wife embraced.

"Thank you," the sad man said to the prince.

"You are welcome," the prince said as he got back up on his horse. He continued along the path.

The prince rode on, but it was only until he found a good place to camp. There was a pond near the place as well as the perfect tree to camp under. The prince made camp and rested.

The next morning, the prince packed up the camp and starting riding again. He had to get to the centre of the forest today and rescue his love. If he did not get there something bad was likely to happen. He went along the path.

The prince had been riding for a couple hours, when he saw an old woman standing on the edge of the path. The prince reined in his horse and stopped near the old woman.

"How far am I from the centre of the forest?" the prince demanded.

"A distance that is long and short," the old woman replied, "Your heart determines the distance you must ride."

"Am I headed in the correct direction?" the prince asked.

"*The heart knows the way,*" *the old woman replied.*

"*If I knew the way, I would not have to stop and ask you,*" *the prince said.*

"*Would you help a poor woman?*" *the old woman asked in a rough voice.*

"*It depends on what help is needed,*" *the prince said.*

"*A dragon stole all my money and now I cannot afford to eat,*" *the old woman said.*

"*I will see if I can find the dragon and get your money back,*" *the prince said as he got down from his horse. He tied the reins to a nearby tree.*

"*Which way did the dragon go?*" *the prince asked.*

"*That way,*" *the old woman pointed into the bush.*

The prince headed in the direction to the old woman pointed. There was very little brush in this area, but the trees grew very close together. Some places the prince had to squeeze between trees to get through. He finally came to a clearing with a cave in it. The prince entered the cave and followed the tunnel. The floor sloped downward, but was not steep. There was a little bit of light from the opening, but that disappeared and the prince found himself walking in the dark. He reached out with his hand and touched the side of the cave to let him know where he was. The tunnel made a few twists and there were a few bends, but otherwise was straight. Slowly the tunnel started to get lighter and the prince could see where he was going. The light got brighter and brighter as the prince continued along the tunnel. This went on until he reached a cavern that was brightly lit. The light reflected off the piles and piles of coins. The cavern was a dozen feet high and about as big across. It was filled with coins and only a small area around the door which was clear. The prince did not see the dragon, but stepped into the cavern. The nearest pile of coins blinked and moved its head to look at him.

"Very rarely does my meal come directly to me," the dragon's voice was deep.

"I am here because you stole money from someone who could not afford it," the prince said, "You need to give it back."

"I do not think I need to do anything," the dragon said, "What are you going to do about it?"

"I challenge you to a battle of riddles," the prince said, "If I win, you let me go with the money you stole."

"I accept that challenge," the dragon said, "What is your first riddle?"

"There are two countries at war with each other," the prince said, "There is a carriage accident with numerous individuals involved in the neutral area between these two countries. In which country do the survivors get buried?"

"Humans do not bury survivors," the dragon answered, "A red house is made with red bricks. A black house is made with black bricks. A grey house is made with grey brick. What is a greenhouse made out of?"

"Glass," the prince answered, "What always runs but never walks, often murmurs, never talks, has a bed but never sleeps, has a mouth but never eats?"

"A river," the dragon replied, "At night they come without being fetched. By day they are lost without being stolen. What are they?"

"The stars," the prince answered, "The more you have of it, the less you see. What is it?"

"Darkness," the dragon replied, "I am always hungry, I must always be fed, the finger I touch, will soon turn red. What am I?"

"Fire," the prince answered, "What is black when you get it, red when you use it, and white when you are all through with it?"

"Charcoal," the dragon replied, "All about, but cannot be seen, can be captured, cannot be held, no throat, but can be heard. What am I?"

"The wind," the prince answered, "If you break me, I do not stop working, if you touch me, I may be snared, if you lose me, nothing will matter. What am I?"

"Your heart," the dragon replied, "I drive men mad, for love of me, easily beaten, never free. What am I?"

"Gold," he prince answered, "Why is a raven like a writing desk?"

The dragon did not answer. His eyes became thoughtful. The prince waited for the dragon's answer. Time passed, but the dragon did not speak. The prince got tired and fell asleep.

When he woke up, the dragon was still deep in thought. The prince ate breakfast. Then he wandered around for a while. Finally he sat back down near the dragon. He ate lunch. As he finished, the prince looked at the dragon. The dragon was still thinking.

"Do you conceit the challenge?" the prince asked.

"Yes," the dragon answered, "I do not know the answer to that riddle. Take the money and leave." The dragon tossed the money pouch to the prince before lying back down. The prince picked up the money pouch and left the cavern. He went back along the tunnel with his hand touched the same wall as when he went down the tunnel.

When he left the cave daylight filtered down through the branches. It seemed to be the same time of day that he had gone into the cave, which meant that he had wasted a day in the search for his love.

The prince went back to where the old woman was waiting for him. He gave her the money pouch.

"Thank you," the old woman said to the prince.

"You are welcome," the prince said as he got back up on his horse. He continued along the path.

The prince rode on. It was half a day later that he saw a young woman standing beside the path. The prince reined in his horse and stopped near the young woman.

"How far am I from the centre of the forest?" the prince demanded.

"A distance that is long and short," the young woman replied, "Your heart determines the distance you must ride."

"Am I headed in the correct direction?" the prince asked.

"The heart knows the way," the young woman replied.

"If I knew the way, I would not have to stop and ask you," the prince said.

"Would you help a woman?" the young woman asked in a silky voice.

"It depends on what help is needed," the prince said.

"An evil witch changed my beloved into a troll," the young woman said, "The only way to change him back is to destroy her power."

"I will see if I can find the evil witch and destroy her power," the prince said as he got down from his horse. He tied the reins to a nearby tree.

"Which way is the evil witch?" the prince asked.

"That way," the young woman pointed into the bush.

The prince headed in the direction the young woman pointed.

He finally came to a clearing with a shack in the middle. The shack was four boards leaning against each other with an fifth board for the roof that was not put on square because it had to let the chimney out of the one corner. There was no sign of a troll or a witch. The door must have been on the other side of the shack because the prince could not see it.

The prince had stopped before entering the clearing. He now stared at the shack and trying to figure out how he ended up here. He was supposed to be looking for his love who had been kidnapped and was being held at the centre of the forest. Every time he stopped to help someone, it took more of his time, and likely farther, away from his love. He needed to stop these distractions and concentrate on finding his love.

The prince turned from the shack and walked back through the forest to where the young woman was waiting.

"Did you destroy her power?" the young woman asked.

"No," the prince answered, "I am searching for the centre of the forest for my love and I need to concentrate on that. I need to find her."

"The way to the centre of the forest is long and short," the young woman's voice changed to what it was the first time she spoke, "Your heart knows the way. Will you not help?"

"I need to find my love," the prince said, "When I find her, I will come back to help you." The prince got up on his horse and turned back to the young woman. In her place was a man who was about fifty years old. His hair and beard had grey and white streaks through them and his stomach stuck out. His shirt and trousers were brown

with a red belt around his waist. His black boots fit snug up to his knees and he held a bag over one shoulder.

"I told you the way was long and short," the man said, "But now the way is closed. The way to the centre of the forest was through your heart. Had you helped get rid of the witch, you would have been closer to your objective. Since you have given up helping, your objective is lost to you."

"Who are you?" the prince asked.

"I am Saint Lang," the man answered, "I am the saint of true and lost love. I tried to help you find your true love, but now you have lost her."

"There is still a chance to get her," the prince said, "All I need is to know how to get to the centre of the forest."

"There is no way into the centre of the forest," Saint Lang answered.

The prince shook his head and rode off. He did not stop for anything, but there were no more people to stop for anyway. He rode and rode. It felt like hours when he finally came to a clearing at the end of the road. In the middle of the clearing lay his love. She was lying on a stone slab in her dress and hair spread out around him. The prince reined in his horse and stopped before sliding off. He knelt down beside her, but she was dead. There was nothing he could do. He kissed her gently before getting back on his horse.

He continued through where there was no road, but it was the opposite direction than he had come and he could not afford to go back and face his love's father after all the promises he had made about bringing her back. He ignored the tree, the branches, and the brush. Nothing stopped him or caused him to slow down. His *horse grew tired, causing him to slow down. But he did not pay attention to anything except his horse's needs.*

The prince rode through the forest as days past. Finally he reached the other side of the forest and stumbled out. This side was a flat valley. There were very few trees and mountains on all sides. Aside from a column of rising smoke in the mountains straight ahead of the prince, there was no sign of humans. The horse stopped and would not go any further no matter how the prince tried to get him to move.

The prince left his horse there and started walking. He walked in the direction of the smoke. He grew tired quickly, but continued to put one foot in front of the other anyway. The field was much bigger than it first appeared and the mountains remained a distance away. The prince walked until he was about equal distance from the forest as he was from the mountain range. He fell to his knees in despair. He saw no reason to live. There was nothing to live for. His life had no purpose without love.

"Saint Lang," the prince screamed, "What is life without love? What is the purpose of living if there is no love?"

Saint Lang appeared in front of the prince.

"You must find your own purpose," Saint Lang answered, "Life without love is still worth living but you must find someone else to live for."

Saint Lang disappeared again. The prince collapsed and blacked out.

The prince woke to his horse nuzzling his shoulder. The prince sat and looked around. He was still in the field with mountains on three sides and the forest on the fourth side. There was no one around, but there was still a column of smoke in front of him. He remembered the loss of his love, but it seemed dim and for away. The feeling of being lost was still there, but there was also the need for action.

Before moving the prince ate some of the rations he had with him. When he was done, the prince cleaned himself off and got up on his horse. Then he rode toward the column of smoke.

It took a day to reach the base of the mountains. The prince and his horse stopped when necessary to rest or eat. There was nothing at the base of the mountains, but the trees started where the slope did. The prince and his horse stopped for the night. Only once both were rested did they start again. The place where they had rested was where two mountains roots met and another could be seen over them. The prince headed up over the roots and into the trees.

Once he was into the trees, the prince found that he could not see very far around him. It was only the feel of the slope that meant he knew that he was going up the hill. And it was levelness of the ground that told him when he had reached the top. This went on for only an hour before he felt the ground slope downward. It was close to noon when he reached the bottom of the slope. Here the trees stopped again and there was another field. At the end of the field was a village with smoke coming from it. He stopped within the tree line and looked toward the village. It was at the base of the mountain and the field was used for farmland. The village had a half built wall around it and the smoke was coming from the ruins of houses, not just chimneys. It looked like something had attacked the village. The prince did not see any people around.

The prince and his horse rested and ate before continuing toward the village. He went across the field without seeing anyone. He reached the wall and found a man working on repairing an area that had marks from claws. The claws marks looked like they came from a dragon. The man was probably in his mid-twenties with thick brown hair and beard. He was wearing work clothes and had a box of tools beside him.

"What village is this?" the prince called. The man looked up from his work and studied the prince. He seemed to be trying to decide whether he could trust the prince with the name of the village. The prince waited for him to speak.

"Mountain Bottom," the man finally answered.

"You must have awfully big cats in this village of Mountain Bottom," the prince commented nodded toward the repairs.

"Ain't cats," the man replied, "It's a dragon. He came and burned up half the village before carrying off the mayor's daughters."

"I have seen no one, except you," the prince said, "Did the dragon scare everyone else away?"

"They are all having a meeting at the pub to figure out what to do about the dragon," the man said, "They never listen to me, so I'm out here doing what I can to be useful."

"And if looks like a very fine job," the prince said.

"If you want to find the rest of them, just go around the wall and find the building on the far side of the village from the fire damage," the man said.

"I hardly think I am going to get anywhere with people who do not listen their own people," the prince said, "Perhaps it is better just to go visit the dragon."

"You won't get far," the man said, "But I wish you good luck."

"Why will I not get far?" the prince asked.

"You have to know the way into the caves," the man answered, "If you do not know the way, you will never find it."

"Do you know the way?" the prince asked.

"I do," the man answered, "But the mayor has forbidden me to enter the caves."

"Why is that?" the prince asked.

"I wish for his daughter's hand in marriage," the man answered, "If I were to rescue her then he would have no choice but to grant it. He does not want a poor worker for a son-in-law and thus has forbidden me to enter the caves."

"In exchange for payment, will you show me the caves?" the prince asked.

"Certainly," the man answered, "But I can't enter them."

"I accept those terms," the prince said.

"Then I will show you the way," the man said. He put down his tools and got to his feet.

"I am Oved," the man said, "What is your name?"

"You can call me Ammon," the prince answered. The man nodded and they started toward the mountain.

The man led the way up to the mountain. When they started up the slope, the prince could see the multitude of caves among the trees. If he had gone alone, he would have never figured out where he should go. The man climbed passed all these caves and up the slope. The prince followed on his horse for a ways, but got down to lead his horse when it got too steep. The man led the way to an area where it appeared that the amount of cave openings had decreased to only one or two. When the prince thought they had run out of caves the man stopped in front of another one.

"Is this the cave?" the prince asked.

"It is," the man answered as he took a torch from just inside the cave and lit it, "However, there will be many tunnels off the main one. You must stay on the main tunnel or you will be lost for days and never find the dragon."

The prince wrapped the reins of his horse around a tree branch before taking the torch from the man. He offered the man a ring off his finger. The man accepted the ring.

"Good luck," the man said.

"Be safe, yourself," the prince said before heading into the cave. The man stood at the opening of the cave as the prince followed the tunnel into the mountains. Only when he turned a corner farther in did the prince no longer see the man. The tunnel was dry and there were occasional bursts of wind from somewhere inside. There was no other light, but the torch. The only sound was the wind and the sound of the prince's footsteps in the dirt floor. There had been debris at the entrance, but the deeper the prince went the less there was. Aside from marks that were likely old footprints, it appeared at that this tunnel was deserted.

The prince had been walking for a while when he came to the first intersection. Two tunnels went off to either side of the main tunnel. The prince did not stray from the main tunnel as he continued. The next several intersections were similar and he followed the main tunnel every time. He was a ways in when he came on an intersection where the main tunnel broke into two *separate tunnels. He stopped and looked at them. They both appeared to be the same one he was walking and there was no sound to indict which to choose. The man had said that he should stay on the main tunnel. The prince studied them again. He found that the one on the left was a smaller opening than the one on the right. The prince went into the tunnel on the right and continued on. He met this type of intersection several times as well as the other type with three tunnels. When there was only two he chose the tunnel with the bigger opening.*

This worked quite well and he got deeper into the mountain and closer to the heart. He was starting to feel the heat that would suggest that was he getting closer to the heart, when he came to another intersection with only two tunnels. He stopped to study them and figure out which one was bigger. Only a few minutes passed before he realized that they were both the same size. He looked them over again, this time for any sign that one was different from the other. There was no sounds coming from either of them and they looked alike. The price started to sigh when he caught the smell of a dragon. He moved closer to the tunnel on the left and sniffed the air. There was no smell, except dirt and rock. He moved to the right tunnel and sniffed again, this time he could smell dragon. He went down that tunnel.

The smell got stronger as he went. There were also sounds starting to reach him. There were claws against rock and the flap of wings. The prince slowed down a little as he tried to walk with less noise. He had drawn his sword, but there was nothing within torch light that was a danger to him. He reached another intersection, but it was obvious which way to go this time. He continued down the tunnel and the smell got stronger and the sounds got closer. Finally he turned a corner and found light coming from the other end of the tunnel. There was also a holder for the torch. The prince placed the torch in the holder and moved to the mouth of the cave. He stopped there and looked out.

This was a cavern big enough for a large dragon with a hole near the top for the dragon to get in and out of. There was a fire to one side with a pot over it. In the centre was a dragon, who was waiting for the pot to boil. It was a young red dragon. A couple more years and the dragon would be an adult with the size, but now it was still a little smaller than that. It was still large to the prince. Close to the pot was a cage suspended from the ceiling with a woman inside it. She looked to be the same age as the man who had helped the prince find the cave. She had long golden hair and a green velvet dress on. She looked scared.

The prince moved quietly into the cave with his sword in hand. Very few men could go up against a young dragon and survive. Most of them were heavily armoured and trained for many years. The prince had no armour, aside from some chainmail, and only basic training.

"Saint Lang," the prince whispered, "If I am meant to fight this dragon and get these two lovers back together, provide me with what I need to fight this dragon."

With that the prince headed toward the dragon. His footfalls were loud enough that the dragon turned to look at him. The dragon inhaled and breathed out a ball of fire. The prince rolled out of the way. When he was up on his feet, he charged at the dragon. The dragon swung its tail and hit the prince, slamming him into the far wall. The prince stayed there a moment to shake his head and clear it. He got to his feet in time to have to roll out of the way of the dragon fire. And he charged. This time when the dragon swung its tail at him, the prince brought his sword down on the dragon's tail. The dragon screeched in pain and withdrew its tail. It breathed fire at him, but he rolled out of the way. This time he was much closer to the dragon. The dragon backed away as he raised his sword again.

The dragon was too focused on him and not what was behind it. The dragon backed into the pot of boiling water and the fire. The fire did not bother the dragon, but the boiling water coming down caused it to cry out in pain. The water also put out the fire and it became dark in the cavern. The only light left was coming from the cave and the torch that was still burning. The dragon was lying there in pain among the ashes of the fire and the hot water.

The prince was careful as he moved toward the dragon. He was watchful of where he put his feet, to avoid hot water or ashes, and he was paying attention for any movement from the dragon. The dragon was crying out in pain, but not moving. The prince reached the dragon's head without it noticing him. The prince swung his sword and put the dragon out of its misery with a blow to the neck.

The prince waited a moment, but the dragon was dead. Once he was sure, the prince went to the wall, where the chain for the cage was attached by a pulley wheel. He pulled the handle to lower the cage that the mayor's daughter was in. Finally it reached the ground. He used the key that was hung beside the pulley wheel to unlocked the cage and let the mayor's daughter out.

"Thank you," the mayor's daughter said.

"We need to get you back," the prince said, "before the people of the village decide to do something about the dragon."

"Very good idea," the mayor's daughter said.

The prince headed for the cave and the mayor's daughter followed him. He grabbed the torch as they went passed it. This time he went faster through the tunnels. He knew the way out and there was something in his gut that told him to hurry. The mayor's daughter was right behind him all the way. She knew this tunnel as well and she must have wanted to get home.

They went through the tunnel at a pace that was just short of a jog. There had been nothing in the tunnel on his way through the first time and there was still nothing in the tunnel on the way through this time. There was just dirt floor, rock walls and ceiling. This time he could hear the mayor's daughter behind him as well as his own footfalls.

They reached the end of the tunnel and the opening into the mountain. The prince put out the torch in the dirt before hanging it back in its holder on the cave wall. The mayor's daughter waited for him.

"We can ride back," the prince said gesturing to his horse, who was still tied to the tree.

The mayor's daughter nodded. She was slight out of breath for the pace, but did not want to slow down. The prince helped her up into the saddle before getting up behind her. The horse seemed to understand that they were in a hurry and moved at a fast pace. They headed down the mountain toward the village. They had to be careful of the caves that were along the mountain. If they were not careful they would end up above one and have to back up to go around it. It took them longer than the prince wanted to get down the mountain side.

Finally they reached the end of the caves and trees, the prince let his horse run as they headed for the village. This time when they reached the wall, the prince directed his horse to go around it and into the village itself. He went around the houses as he slowed his horse down. Finally they reached the village square. All the men of the village were gathered there and they all had weapons with them. Between two men was the man who had helped the prince and the mayor was standing over the man with a sword raised. The prince could tell it was the mayor because he not only wore the chain of office, but he also had the most expensive clothing.

"Halt," the prince commanded. Everyone stopped and looked over at the prince. They all looked surprised at him and the mayor's daughter.

"Explain yourselves," the prince commanded as he got off his horse.

"I am the mayor of this village," the mayor said, "and we are just dealing with a thief." The prince saw the ring he had given the man on the mayor's finger.

"That man is no thief," the prince said, "I paid him the ring to help me."

"You paid him?" the mayor asked.

"Of course," the prince answered, "I asked him to help me find the dragon. He showed me the way to the caves, but could not guide me the rest of the way. So, I paid him and followed his directions to get the rest of the way."

"You defeated the dragon?" one of the villagers holding the man asked.

"*He did,*" the mayor's daughter declared from on the prince's horse.

"*We are in your debt,*" the mayor said with a slight bow, "*We will certainly reward you grandly.*" The mayor glanced briefly at his daughter.

"*Wonderful,*" the prince said, "*I love watching weddings.*" The prince slapped the mayor heartily on the back. "*And I am sure that you are proud to call Oved your future son-in-law.*" The village cheered while the mayor swallowed his reply. He was not happy, but there was nothing he could do about. The villagers released Oved and he rushed over to the mayor's daughter. He helped her off the prince's horse and into his arms. She hugged him back. The kiss sent the villagers cheering all over again. The prince smiled as he held out his hand. The mayor removed the ring and handed it to the prince. The prince watched Oved and the mayor's daughter and felt happiness well up in his heart. He remembered his love in his heart and not in his head. The world felt right again.

The wedding took place the next day with a flurry of activity all night. The prince was given some place to rest while everyone else prepared the food and the clothing. At the wedding, the bride looked radiate in the gown that had been found for her and the groom looked happy in the suit that was a size too big. The men of the village were organizing a work crew for the next day to try and build a house for the newlyweds as a wedding gift since there had not been time to get any other gifts together. The prince enjoyed the wedding, stayed for the feast, and then left after giving the bride and groom his best wishes.

He got on his horse and rode out of town. He went a little distance from the village and stopped to look back.

"Perhaps that is what my purpose is," the prince said, "To make sure that other true loves do get together."

"That is a good purpose," Saint Lang said from where he was sitting in the grass watching the sun. The prince smiled with this new found knowledge before turning his horse away from the village. He rode off into the sunset in search of others who needed his help.

The old man's voice stopped with the end of the story and Zebulon felt his eyes drift closed. Sleep came over him.

ZEBULON FINDS HIS PURPOSE AND COMES UP WITH A PLAN

It was still dark when Zebulon woke up. He sat up and looked around. Nothing had changed. He was still sitting at the empty fountain and the old man was still sitting nearby. He looked over at the old man.

"Is there really a Saint Lang?" Zebulon asked.

"As far as I know." the old man answered, "Stories are not always fiction."

"Does he actually help those who have lost their loves to find a purpose for their life again?" Zebulon asked.

"As far as I know," the old man answered.

"Are you hungry?" Zebulon asked as he got to his feet.

"Always," the old man answered.

"Come on," Zebulon said, "I know a good place to get food."

"Wonderful," the old man said as he got to his feet. He followed Zebulon as Zebulon started up the street.

Zebulon knew where he was because he had come to this part of the city once with his father to deal with a problem. He followed the route he knew while being careful of the guards. They had ignored him during his wandering, but now he appeared to have a destination and the old man following him, Zebulon was not sure that they would continue that practice. The old man followed him up through the poor section without a word. He followed Zebulon up through the middle class section with only a slight hesitation. When they reached the upper class neighbourhood, the old man stopped. Zebulon had gone a few steps before he realized that the old man was not behind him. He turned back.

"What is wrong?" Zebulon asked.

"If you are caught in this section, the guards beat you," the old man answered.

"We will not be caught." Zebulon said, "We can go a different way through this section."

"All right," the man said, "but I am likely to die if I am beaten for trespassing."

"You are not trespassing." Zebulon said, "The streets are not privately owned."

"Explain that to the people," the old man said.

Zebulon did not say anything to that, but the led the way to a section of alley ways that were used by servants. Due to the time of night, there was no one else going through there. The old man felt more comfortable in the confines of the alley ways than the open of the streets and always hesitated if they had to cross a street to get from one alley way to another. They made their way through the zigzags of the alley ways to the street across from the wall around the castle itself. All the three gates were open and there were no guards posted at the gates. They could be closed to keep people out, but Zebulon had never wanted that much distance between himself and the people. The only people who ever suggested closing them were some of the nobles in court who would rather not be near the people of the city. Zebulon had ignored such comments and waved away their ignorance. It now showed his own ignorance at the fact that he had accepted their views by not correcting them on the value of human life no matter what class the person was.

The vision of Angus and Orestes laughing as their carriage ran over the woman who Zebulon loved, overcame Zebulon and it took a minute before he noticed a tap on his shoulder. The old man looked at him with concern. Zebulon shrugged the vision off and started across the street. There was no one in sight so the old man followed behind him. They went across the street and into the nearest gate. The court yard was silent as they passed through it like shadows. Zebulon led the way to the kitchen door. He knocked on it.

A minute past before it opened. The ovens were going and the cooking had been started for the day. Zebulon made no attempt to get inside but stood there. The head cook looked him over and then looked the old man over. Then he went back inside and the door closed behind him. The old man turned to leave, but Zebulon stopped him. As the old man turned back the door opened. The head cook held out a bowl of scraps. Zebulon took it and bowed his head in thanks. The head cook closed the door. Zebulon and the old man went to the alcove that was beside the kitchen door. They sat down on the cobblestones and ate out of the bowl.

As he ate, Zebulon felt like this was the best food he had ever had in his life. There was nothing better than good food after days of not eating. The old man seemed to enjoy the food the same as he did. Finally the scraps were gone and both sat back with full stomachs.

"So, what is my purpose?" Zebulon asked, "What would you say it is, Saint Lang? Especially now that I have lost the only thing worth living for?"

"You are the king." the old man answered, "Your purpose is to rule over these people, to protect them from harm, and to produce an heir that can be taught those same things. You are King Zebulon of Proster, just as I am Saint Lang. Your love must be for your kingdom, just as the prince in the story learned to love the people who needed his help."

"I cannot protect my own people." Zebulon said, "The death of the woman I loved proved that. She would still be alive, if not for me. I did not even get to know her name."

"You can protect your people," Saint Lang said, "especially now that you know the dangers. You are the king. You have a responsibility to the people. Love your people because they were her people as well. She was one of the people you are the king over. Love them because she was one of them."

Zebulon was silent as he thought about it. He found his eyes closing and his head dropping forward.

"You have a duty to your people," Saint Lang's voice was soft in Zebulon's thoughts.

Zebulon woke up to the sun peeking around the wall of the alcove. He blinked the sleep out of his eyes and looked around. Saint Lang was gone, but where he had been was a medallion with his symbol on it. Zebulon picked it up and slipped it over his head. He tucked it into this shirt before getting to his feet. He picked up the bowl before leaving the alcove. It was the middle of the afternoon and people were out and about in the court yard. None of them glanced in his direction. Zebulon went back to the kitchen door. He opened it and stepped inside. Everyone inside was working on supper. The staff looked at him, but he ignored them. He put the bowl on the counter with the rest of the dishes to be washed before heading to the door that went to the rest of the castle. Zebulon walked the halls to the staircase that took him up to the tower. The few servants he passed gave him strange looks, but no one tried to stop him. When he reached the stairs, Zebulon went up them. At the top of the tower, he stopped at the window and looked out. He studied the city for several minutes before taking out his spyglass. He searched the market place for the vegetable stall but did not find it.

Zebulon supposed that she would not be there because of how soon it was after her daughter's death. She might also be having trouble because she did not have any help. Zebulon wondered if he could send her help, or money that would make her life easier.

There was the sound of someone coming up the stairs and they sounded like they were coming up with speed. Zebulon put the spyglass away. He was not sure why he put it away, but he figured that it must have been an automatic reflex. No one would know what he was looking for with the spyglass because it was not there anymore.

Dard came up the finally stairs. He looked happy to see Zebulon until he saw the expression on Zebulon's face.

"What happened?" Dard asked while trying to get his breath back.

"It did not work out," Zebulon answered, "I never got to talk to her."

"What happened?" Dard asked.

"She is dead," Zebulon answered.

"Oh," Dard's voice was quiet before he fell silent. He stood there without speaking as he thought that piece of news over. Zebulon refused any thought that wanted to come into his head. He was better off without them. They would just mess him up.

"Now what?" Dard finally broke the silence.

"I need you to ask around and find out who her mother is," Zebulon answered, "then you will get her the help she needs to survive."

"I will do that as soon as possible," Dard said.

"Also, I want to know who Orestes is and why he is spending so much time at court," Zebulon said.

"I will try," Dard said.

"Have you found out anything about the conspiracy to kill me?" Zebulon asked.

"No," Dard answered, "most people have been too busy wondering where you went to discuss plans of domination."

"Has anything come of the investigation into the death of Gaius's assistant?" Zebulon asked.

"Sort of." Dard answered, "Martin's body has gone missing. Garrick has searched everywhere, so that it could be returned home, but it is gone. Garrick is searching the whole castle all over again in case he missed it the first time. Gaius is even more upset over the disappearance of the body. It appears as if he is truly upset over it and not just to hide something. Garrick has not uncovered anything else that I know of. He has been unwilling to talk about it to anyone."

"Anything else happen while I was gone?" Zebulon asked.

"No," Dard answered, "That was pretty much everything."

"How is Thalia?" Zebulon asked.

"Still suspicious that I am worthy of being in the same room as her, but she is warming up to me." Dard said, "It is going slow."

"She will figure out that you are worth it," Zebulon said.

"How do you know?" Dard asked.

"I am the king," Zebulon answered, "I just know these things."

"Yeah, right." Dard said, "I will get on those requests for information." Dard headed back down the stairs. Zebulon stayed up there gazing over the whole city.

He was responsible to all those people, who were living their lives in peace. It was his duty to provide an heir who would also protect that peace. Without the woman he loved, providing the world with an heir would be difficult. Of course, any woman in the city would be willing to provide the king with an heir. He could also adopt a child who needed a home, but after Zebulon was gone there would be nobility who would dispute his right to the throne. He could pick a woman off the streets, who needed a home, and marry her. That would help someone in need and he would have a legitimate heir. The other option was to marry someone at court, but right now he had no interest in anyone there.

He also had to survive to produce an heir, which meant he would have to do something about the diplomats and their treaties. He wanted nothing to do with the portraits they brought. He had to find some excuse to send them home and demand that no one be sent in their place, without it resulting in war. This was going to take some thought.

The sound of someone else coming up the stairs came to Zebulon. He waited until he could see them. It was the castle steward.

"Yes?" Zebulon asked.

"Herwin and Garrick would like to meet with you once you feel like being king again." the steward answered, "Shall I run a bath for you?"

"As long as you can guarantee me that there will be nothing in it that will kill me," Zebulon answered.

"I will do my best," the steward said. He turned and went back down the stairs. Zebulon thought he could hear the sound of a cloak brushing over stones. He looked around the tower, but there was no one up here. Zebulon shook his head and went back to staring out the window. The sound of the castle steward going down the stairs was the only thing that Zebulon could hear now and there was nothing unusual about that.

Zebulon stayed up there thinking about his plan for a while longer. Finally he headed back down the stairs. He did not meet anyone coming up the stairs. He went through the hallways without being stopped. He reached his bed chamber to find the castle steward finishing up the arrangement for his bath.

"I believe it is safe," the steward told Zebulon before leaving the room. The steward closed the door behind him. Zebulon locked it before getting ready for his bath.

Zebulon felt better now that he was clean, but he still did not feel like going out and being the king of Proster. But he told the steward that he was willing to meet with Herwin and Garrick anyway. Zebulon went to his office and sat down at his desk. There were no traps, but there was a pile of paper work waiting for him. He started with the top one while he waited for Herwin and Garrick. It took half an hour before there was a knock at the door.

"Come in," Zebulon called. The door opened and his advisors stepped into his office. Garrick closed the door behind them.

"What are the results of your investigation?" Zebulon asked.

"I am still working on it," Garrick answered.

"Then what do you two want?" Zebulon asked.

"We are worried," Herwin answered, "for you and for this kingdom. There are dangers that come with being king."

"I am aware of the dangers that go with being king." Zebulon rose and looked at them while his voice rose with every sentence, "I have been dealing with being king and everything that goes with it. I am aware that as king I have certain duties. I am also aware that both of you would have me locked away in a room and protected from the harsh realities of the world. As king, I do not have the luxury of ignoring any of those realities. I am not my father, but I am of his blood. I can fight my own battles. I learned from him and have developed my own abilities. If either of you do not like how I run my kingdom, then you can go back to your estates and stay there. I appreciate your advice, but only when I ask for it. I do not need you to tell me things I already know, or keep things from me that I need to know. Am I being clear?"

"Yes," Garrick said. Herwin was silent. Zebulon glared at him. Herwin broke eye contact first.

"Yes," his voice was quiet.

"Now, is there anything else?" Zebulon asked.

"Yes," Garrick answered, "the harsh realities of being king." Garrick took out a bundle of papers and offered them to Zebulon. Zebulon took them and flipped through them. They were all reports of incidents involving Angus and peasants in the market place.

"We did not want to bother you with them because it was just minor stuff," Garrick said, "but there is a report that he may have killed someone."

"I will deal with it." Zebulon said, "Anything else?"

"No," Garrick said.

"Then you are dismissed," Zebulon said. Herwin and Garrick left the office and closed the door behind them. Zebulon sat back down in his chair and started going through the papers that Garrick had given him.

After breakfast the next day, instead of going into the throne room, Zebulon went out on the balcony at the front of the castle that was used for special occasions and announcements. A lady was out there. She had long hair the colour of soft leather, a gown of turquoise, and white skin that could only be achieved through being trapped indoors. Zebulon thought he had seen her at the back in court a couple time. He walked to the rail.

"Beautiful day, is it not?" Zebulon asked.

"It is, Your Majesty," the lady said with a curtsy. Her eyes were a match to her dress. He would have called her beautiful, but she was a shallow comparison to the woman he had loved.

"You are Lady Thalia, correct?" Zebulon asked.

"That is correct." Thalia answered, "I am surprised you know who I am."

"Dard talks about you all the time." Zebulon said, "He claims you are the most beautiful woman at court, but since you are rarely at court, I was taking his word for it."

"And now that you have seen me up close?" Thalia asked. She titled her head as the corners of her mouth lifted in a slight smile.

"It hardly seems to be a good idea to get between someone and the thing they admire so fiercely," Zebulon answered. The corners of her mouth slipped down and there was a puzzled look in her eyes.

"I am surprised to find you at the castle." Zebulon said, "I did not call court today."

"I like the view from up here." Thalia said, "I came for the view. Many times I come to go to court and end up out here looking over the city. That is why you do not see me in court very often. You do not come out here much."

"No, I do not," Zebulon said, "but I have been learning about different perspectives lately and decided to see what this one was like."

"Are these perspectives changing your view at all?" Thalia asked.

"You think my view needs changing?" Zebulon asked.

"Perhaps it is not my place," Thalia said.

"Very few members of my court expressions their views on my behaviour." Zebulon said, "The only one so far that is willing to speak up is Dard. I would truly like to hear your view. You need not fear repercussions."

"You have had a very narrow perspective." Thalia said, "You let people behave how they wish, not to your own morals. The people gather in court to be important, but they are useless people. The diplomats believe that you are easy to push over. Some have referred to you as a figure head rather than a king. You did not take charge, but let them all go passed you. It is like you do not care and the people are suffered for it. Certain nobles abuse the people you should be protecting because they believe you will do nothing about it and they have that right as nobility. People are people and all are deserving of respect."

"You sound like Dard," Zebulon said.

"Dard clings to the party group to make himself more important than he is." Thalia said, "I have never seen him care for anything aside from himself."

"He told me that you care more for status and possessions than people." Zebulon said, "I think you are both making wrong impressions on each other. I appreciate your honesty and I think you are correct in your assessment."

"Then what are you going to do about?" Thalia asked.

"Pay attention to what people are doing in my kingdom." Zebulon answered, "So, that I can make changes to not only stop that behaviour, but prevent from happening again."

"It is a very ambitious goal," Thalia said.

"But very necessary," Zebulon said.

"I am glad to hear that," Thalia said.

"Thank you for this discussion." Zebulon said, "I thought I wanted to be alone, but apparently what I needed was to hear someone else's opinion."

"You are welcome," Thalia said.

"I will leave you to your view," Zebulon said. Thalia curtsied and Zebulon went back inside.

Zebulon headed for his office when he heard a scream. He rushed back to the balcony. Thalia was on the ground while Dard was grappling with a man in black cloak. Zebulon went through the doors and rushed to help Dard. He grabbed the man's throat from behind. The man's hold on Dard loosen. Dard got one arm free and punched the man. The man went limp. Zebulon slowly let go and the man collapsed to the ground. Dard rubbed his hand.

"Thanks you for your help," Dard said, "I was following him and I saw him try to push Thalia off the balcony."

The man suddenly bolted for the door into the castle. Zebulon made a grab for his cloak, but missed. Dard was also too slow to get him. The man was gone when Zebulon tried to follow him into the castle. Zebulon went back to Dard.

"Who was it?" Zebulon asked.

"I think it was Luce," Dard answered, "but I never saw his face."

Zebulon nodded to himself.

"You better go see to Thalia," Zebulon said glancing at Thalia, who was still sitting on the ground in shock. Dard nodded before turning his back on Zebulon.

Zebulon went back into the castle. He searched around the doorway and down the halls a little bit. There was no trace of the man. Zebulon finally gave up and headed for his office. He had a lot of paperwork to deal with.

ZEBULON'S PLAN IS PUT INTO ACTION BECAUSE OF OTHER PEOPLE'S ACTIONS AGAINST HIM

It was the middle of the afternoon when he finally ran out of paperwork. He had skipped lunch in favour of working and had not eaten. He pushed his chair back and reflected on how he felt. He was a little hungry, happy to have the work done, but there was still the hole that should have been filled with love.

Before Zebulon could delve deeper into that feeling, there came a knock at the door.

"Come in," Zebulon called. The door opened and Dard stepped inside. Dard closed the door before taking a seat.

"How is Thalia?" Zebulon asked.

"A little bruised and shaky, but otherwise fine." Dard answered, "She is likely to start having a guard with her at all times for a while. The person stopped and watched you talk to her. Only when you left did he try to attack her. I think it might have something to do with the fact that you do not usually talk to women alone. They thought you might be interested in her and thus they had to prevent you from getting together with her."

"Then I shall have to keep my distance." Zebulon said, "I had not meant to talk to anyone this morning, but she happened to be out there at the time. She does not deserve to be dragged into this mess. Did you find any of the information I was looking for?"

"Yes," Dard said, "I found the woman's mother. She is currently living off what was left of the money donated to her through the undertaker. The woman's body was buried properly and everything before any money came to her, but that was all right. She refused any offer of help. She intends to bring the matter before the court and demand punishment of the man whose carriage it was."

"Lord Breton has been sick for several years," Zebulon said, "only his son could have been in the carriage at the time. If she brings it before the court, I will hear her out and punish the ones who deserve it. Anything else that you have found?"

"Orestes does not appear to be of nobility." Dard said, "He matches the description of the missing servant of Lord Gunter, The servant has been missing only a short time before Orestes showed up in court. Lord Gunter does not make it to court, so that is the best place for Orestes to hide. Also Lord Gunter had a son that died when he was about Orestes age and it is believed that some of the son's clothes disappeared when Orestes did."

"What is Orestes relationship with Angus like?" Zebulon asked.

"Orestes is friends with Angus on the basis that Angus provides him with a place to stay." Dard answered, "Overall, Angus seems to be hiding Orestes, though I cannot find a reason why he would do that."

"Probably has some view on how it benefits him." Zebulon said, "Anything more on the conspiracy to kill me? Aside from it is likely that Luce is the third conspirator."

"Not much," Dard said, "I was hoping to find out more, but I think I might have given myself away when I helped Thalia on the balcony."

"Then use your sources of information rather than doing it yourself." Zebulon said, "I need that information."

"I will," Dard said.

"Anything else?" Zebulon asked.

"Not at the moment," Dard said as he stood up, "I will find you when I have some more information."

"Okay," Zebulon said. Dard left the office.

Zebulon cleaned up his desk and looked around. There were a few other things that he should do, but he really did not feel like doing any of them. Instead he got up and left his office. With his brain on automatic, Zebulon wandered the halls until he reached the staircase and he followed it up. He reached the tower and looked out over the city. He did not have his spyglass with him today and really did not want it anyways. Instead he turned and slumped down against the wall. And there he stayed.

Zebulon was not sure how long he sat there, but the coldness had seeped from the stones into his body, which was crying for him to move. But he did not move, nor did he let any thought dominate in his head. He cared not for dwelling on the death of the woman he had loved, but he did not care about figuring out a reason to go on living. Because by his standards, there were no more reasons to keep living, especially if his existence was putting other people in danger.

The sound of footsteps came to him. The footsteps were soft and the person was much closer to the top than when he usually heard them. The person who came into sight was Luce wrapped in his usual black cloak. Zebulon thought that Luce might be here to kill him, but if it was so then that was the way things would go.

Luce came all the way up the stairs and then moved to the wall opposite Zebulon. He sat down and leaned against the wall.

"It took me a long time to figure out where you went when you disappeared." Luce said, "If I had not been following the castle steward, I would never have found it. Few people in this castle know about the stairs and those that do know about it do not know where it goes." Luce looked around the small area that was the landing. He noticed the door, but his attention was to the symbol that was on it.

"I have not seen that symbol in a while," Luce said, "not since my father banned all mages from Wodend. It used to be very common for wizards and the like to carve into burial places for other wizards. It seems to be a strange place for it to be on a door in the tower."

"My father killed the wizard." Zebulon said, "He probably did not want anyone to mess with the body or the magical components."

"He was a wise man then." Luce said, "I have seen the results of many people who have used magic without knowledge. It is never a good result."

"Are you a magic user?" Zebulon asked.

"I was," Luce answered, "I still use minor amounts. The problem with being a magic user is that the large source of magic in this part of the world seems to have dried up. That is why I agreed to come here as a diplomat. The portal with which the magic flowed was in

Proster. I had hoped to discover the reason behind the loss of magic."

"I have no knowledge of magic." Zebulon said, "My father did, but you are too late to ask him."

"I have done some searching, but have not discovered the reason." Luce said, "I believe it would take finding the portal. Since I have not had much maneuverability to do such, I have not found it."

"Perhaps the portal is gone," Zebulon said, "and with it the magic."

"That is possible." Luce said, "As soon as I am done here, I will be going to search for another source of magic."

"You can leave anytime." Zebulon said, "You have not brought forward any treaties from Wodend."

"I have a treaty from my king for you," Luce said as he pulled a scroll out of his cloak and rolled it across the floor to Zebulon. Zebulon picked it and unrolled it. He read it through. It said that Proster and Wodend would not go to war against each other, would leave trade open for those merchants who wished to trade, and otherwise would be allies if there was ever a war. There were no clauses that were suspicious, or extra wordy and all of it could be understood easily. Zebulon read it through again.

"I will have to do the official signing of it later," Zebulon said, "but the portrait you brought, you can take home with you."

"I figured that," Luce said, "and I hardly blame you for it. It would be better for you to marry from within Proster and not from the neighbouring kingdoms. The lady has been a problem to her father because anyone who knows her will not marry her and she has gained a large reputation. That makes her a very bad catch for you. However, given all that, there are a few other reasons to stay."

"Like what?" Zebulon asked.

"For one," Luce said, "I have Martin staying in my rooms. I would return his body for Garrick to finish his investigation, but Martin is busy using it."

"I thought he was poisoned?" Zebulon asked.

"He was, but it was merely a sleeping potion." Luce answered, "It made him appear dead for a day, but then he woke up. I happened to be snooping around when he woke up. He seemed very concerned about his situation and begged to be given refuge in my rooms. I smuggled him inside and he has been hiding there ever since. Garrick has searched the castle, but refuses to search my rooms even when I have offered to let him. I can try to get him to come out, if it will be helpful."

"He can stay there as long as he wants to." Zebulon said, "I am more interested in what he is scared of."

"I believe he is scared of Gaius, Atius, and Jarlan." Luce said, "They have poisons. One of them is bound to be the one he drank. I'm just not sure why they would give it to Martin, unless it was to test it out. Though he could have drank it by accident. You are aware that they are planning on killing you."

"They have made several attempts at killing me." Zebulon said, "None have succeeded so far."

"You have more will to live than I have." Luce said, "I would likely have fallen victim to them already."

"I thought I had something to live for," Zebulon said.

"You have a lot to live for." Luce said, "You have to show those three that you are not a push over. You have to defend your kingdom in the name of your father and your descendants."

"What do you live for?" Zebulon asked.

"Magic," Luce answered.

"And when you found the source gone, what did you do?" Zebulon asked.

"I grieved for it," Luce said, "then I decided to find out why. If I fail that then I have to find a new source."

"All I have is ruling a kingdom." Zebulon said, "That is not much of a life."

"Then you need to find someone, through whom you can live vicariously." Luce said, "I accept certain things because of my magic. I will never find love. Everywhere I go, magic is looked down upon and as such none of the women have an interest in me. My life will be shorter than anyone else's because I use some of my life force in the magic. Hard work and time in the sun are too harsh for me, even when I believe that I could do something involving both of them. These are all things that were lost to me the moment that I started experimenting with magic. I have found people who can do those things and I get them to talk to me about them. In those moments, I can love, live forever, do hard work, and spend time in the sunshine."

"I will have to think about that," Zebulon said.

"What did you lose?" Luce asked.

"Love," Zebulon answered.

"That is the hardest to live without," Luce said, "but people do it all the time. What you need to do is find the best deal to get an heir. Do not pick anyone outside your own kingdom, it will make everything worse."

"I was not planning to look outside my own kingdom." Zebulon said, "Most of the treaties seem to be excuses to come into my kingdom and try to kill me. I understand why Jarlan wants me out of the way. Grackle would love to take over Proster. I just cannot understand why Atius and Gaius are going along with him."

"Lithimin and Sendal are in need of trade with Grackle." Luce said, "I think the plan was in place before they were sent from their kingdoms. It sounded like Wodend was offered an in, but the king refused it. If Proster became part of Grackle, Wodend would have more problems than if Proster was remain as it is now. Once Grackle has Proster, they are going to work at getting the Sendal as their next territory with Lithimin after that. When they have all that, their attention will turn to Wodend. We do not have that kind of military."

"I do not plan on losing Proster to Grackle." Zebulon said, "If my father wanted to give it up, he would have done it shortly after he took it over. Since he did not do that, I will defend it against Grackle. As far as I know they do not have the military to openly attack anyway. I am going to have to create the treaties with them and send the three of them home. I just have to do it carefully."

"Prove that they are trying to kill you," Luce said, "then they have to accept the terms of your treaty and go home. If you phrase things right in the treaty, those kingdoms cannot send more diplomats"

"The problem is proving that they are the ones trying to kill me." Zebulon said, "I have covered up ever attempt so far, which has worked in their favour."

"Well, now you know not to cover it up." Luce said, "I am sure that they will try again and you will get your proof from that."

"I just have to survive the attempts," Zebulon said.

"You have been able to do it so far." Luce said, "As long as you are wary of your surroundings and watchful of people, you should do fine."

"As usual," Zebulon said.

Neither man spoke as they sat there. Zebulon stared at the floor in front of him and Luce stared at the door.

"Did you notice when the source of magic disappeared?" Luce asked, "Anything different that you noticed?"

"We did have some problems with demons while my father was alive," Zebulon said, "but there was not much else around here that involve magic. My father disliked magic and discouraged magic users."

"Then how did he deal with demons?" Luce asked.

"He fought them," Zebulon answered, "and won. He had a sword he called, The Wizard Slayer. It worked quite well against any kind of magic. It disappeared years ago about the same time as the demons did. I have no idea what happened to it."

"What demon was he chasing?" Luc asked.

"He called it a collector," Zebulon answered.

"I have heard of them, but I do not really know much about them." Luce said, "I do know however that they usually are not much of threat to anyone."

"He was a threat in Proster because he was kidnapping children." Zebulon said, "My father went after him and brought the children back. The sword did not come back with him and my youngest sister disappeared about that time. We have not had a problem with demons ever since."

"Do you know anything else about what happened?" Luce asked.

"He never talked about," Zebulon answered, "and no one really asked. He was a warrior and if something happened that was bad enough that he would not talk about it, then no one else wanted to know."

"That is understandable," Luce said.

"One of the assassins that was sent after me used magic." Zebulon said, "He called himself a Reeze. How is he able to be here if the source of magic is dried up?"

"The Reeze works on different principles than any other magic." Luce said, "The only thing I am surprised about is that he did not succeed."

"He said he refused to fulfill the agreement because of the white wolf." Zebulon said, "The white wolf has been warning me about dangers, but I do not know anything about her."

"It is rare for an animal to take it upon itself the job of protecting a human," Luce said, "and those are usually because of a developed bond. A white wolf with magical ability is a strange occurrence and probably a very powerful ally for you."

"I am willing to take all the allies I can get," Zebulon said, "especially if that is the type of help I get."

"Her appearing suggested that the wolf is somehow its own source of magic." Luce said, "That could mean that she is likely a shape-shifter. Most of them are elves or the like and have the innate magic that means they do not need an actual source of magic. But one powerful enough to stop a Reeze from going through with an agreement; I would love to meet such a being."

"I have not met with the white wolf physically." Zebulon said, "So, I cannot introduce you."

"That is okay." Luce said, "Knowing that there is such a creature and that they can come to here is enough. If the wolf can visit you and protect you, then magic is not completely gone. That is great news for me, especially with my current search."

"As soon as the treaties are signed, you have my permission to search for what happened to the source of magic." Zebulon said, "I have no problems with it. If you find anything that might be interested to my family, I would appreciate knowing about."

"If it is applicable to your family, I would not keep it from you," Luce said.

There was the sound of footsteps coming up the stairs. Luce looked at Zebulon with one eyebrow raised. Zebulon looked back and shrugged.

"People wander around here all the time." Zebulon said, "I have never said that people cannot come up here. I just do not advertise its existence. The only people that usually come up here are Dard and the castle steward."

"Yes, Dard, I have been meaning to talk to you about him." Luce said, "Mainly the request that he stop trying to follow me around."

"I can ask to him to," Zebulon said, "but he thinks you were the one who tried to push Thalia off the balcony."

"Thalia is one of the nobles?" Luce asked

"A noblewoman who makes it to court occasionally." Zebulon answered, "Dard likes her."

"I have not been trying to push noblewomen off of balconies." Luce said, "I have other things to do. Why would anyone want to push her off?"

"Our belief is that the man saw me talking to her and decided to kill her," Zebulon said, "but since we have not found and identified the man, it is hard ask him why he did it."

"Maybe it was Myles," Luce said, "trying to get you interested in the many portraits he brought with him. After all he has not been trying to kill anyone yet."

"He was too tall to be Myles," Zebulon said, "even if Myles was wearing lifts."

"That leaves three others diplomats," Luce said.

"And a whole court of nobles." Zebulon said, "A few of them seem to have an amoral streak."

"I have not been paying as much attention to the members of your court." Luce said, "Most of them seem more concerned with status than power or anything else."

"They are, but apparently the loss of the lives of peasants are meaningless to them," Zebulon said, "and that is a very bad thing. It is problem that I have to deal here soon."

"One of the many problems that kings have to deal with," Luce said.

The castle steward came into view and then reached the top of the stairs. Both Zebulon and Luce looked up at him.

"Pardon me, but the head cook is looking for you, Sire," the castle steward said.

"What is it about?" Zebulon asked.

"Dard," the steward answered.

"Where is he?" Zebulon asked as he scrambled to his feet.

"The store room," the steward answered before stepping out of the way and letting Zebulon passed.

Zebulon took the stairs two at a time. At the bottom of the stairs, he ran down the hallways to the store room. He opened the door and found the head cook standing over the cot that was kept in there. Dard was lying on the cot. There was a bit of blood in the side of his mouth and his skin was white. There was no other sign of anything wrong.

"What happened?" Zebulon asked.

"I opened a bottle of wine to serve with supper." the head cook was trembling, "I poured a taste for myself and a taste for Dard. He took the first sip because someone in the kitchen was yelling for me."

Zebulon could see the bottle and two glasses set out on a nearby barrel. One was empty and the other had a small amount of red wine in it.

"Immediately he started convulsing," the head cook continued, "I was not sure what else to do, so I got him to lie down and sent for you."

"Looks like poison," Luce said from behind Zebulon.

"Do you know what to do about it?" Zebulon asked.

"I can figure it out," Luce said. He went to the barrel. He sniffed at the glass.

"Moa root." Luce said, "Effective, painful, and very rare. Hopefully the universal antidote works. Can I get a glass of water?"

"I will get it," the head cook said before leaving the room.

Zebulon kneeled down beside Dard. His breathing sounded wrong, his skin was cold, and his eyes had lost their focus.

"How long does the poison take to work?" Zebulon turned to Luce. Luce was examining the bottle without touching it.

"It paralyzes the person," Luce said, "which suffocates them. Dard has about five more minutes to live, if he does not get the antidote. The cook must have left the bottle out and the poison was injected into it through the cork."

"Here is the water," the head cook arrived back in the store room. He was barely able to stop it from spilling. Luce took it and extracted a small vial from his cloak. He took the top off the vial with his teeth before putting three drops of the liquid into the cup of water. Then Luce handed the cup to Zebulon. Zebulon carefully got Dard into a sitting position before he started pouring the water down Dard's throat. He did not stop until all the water was gone. Zebulon let Dard's body slid back down to the bed. Zebulon set the cup down on the nearest barrel and focused on Dard. A minute passed before Dard's breathing went to normal and his skin regained it colour.

"What does moa root look like?" Zebulon asked Luce.

"It is a green root usually about an inch wide and three inches long," Luce showed the dimensions with his fingers, "and has to be kept in a jar or glass bottle. When made into tea, which is usually how it is used, it is a clear green liquid."

"Stay with him and send someone for me if his condition changes." Zebulon told the head cook, "I am not worried about supper. Get the rest to feed the servants that show up, but make sure that the food has not been left alone at any point in time."

"Yes, sire," the head cook said.

"Come with me." Zebulon told the castle steward, "You as well, Luce, if you want."

"I have been here through most of this," Luce said, "I might as well see the end of it."

Zebulon led the way out of the store room. He headed to the throne room. It was empty except for the two guards at the doorway.

"You follow me," Zebulon pointed to the one on the right before turning to the one on the left, "You get the guards to gather everyone in the castle, except the castle's servants, in the throne room. Use force if you have to."

"Yes, Your Majesty," the guards said.

Zebulon turned and headed up the stairs to the area where the guest chambers were. Everyone else followed him.

They stopped at the first door and Zebulon knocked on it. A moment passed before the door opened. Myles stood there in pants and bare feet.

"What can I do for Your Majesty?" Myles said with a bow.

"Get dressed and go down to the throne room," Zebulon said.

"You wish to hold court?" Myles asked.

"I am going to search your rooms," Zebulon answered.

"Just one moment," Myles said before bowing again. He left the door open as he disappeared from sight.

"Get dressed," Myles voice was quiet. There were the sounds of two people getting dressed. Then Myles and the youngest daughter of Lord Menawa exited the room without looking at any of the people standing aside to let them pass.

"We are looking for moa root." Zebulon said as they entered the room, "It should be in a jar. Looks like a green root, or green water."

Zebulon, Luce, the castle steward, and the guard took an area and started to search.

Ten minutes later they were done without finding any moa root. They left the room. Out in the hallway, the guards were escorting people down to the throne room. People gave Zebulon and group curious looks. They whispered among themselves, but Zebulon ignored it and continued to the next door.

The group searched all the rooms one at a time. All the people had been cleared out. There was no moa root in Jarlan's room, but there was a scroll that had instructions on how to create moa root tea. There was no moa root in Atius's room, but there was a kettle with traces of the tea. The vial of moa root tea was in Gaius's room.

But Zebulon continued to Luce's room.

"You want to search it?" Luce asked.

"I want to talk to Martin," Zebulon answered.

"I understand," Luce said and wave his hand over the knob before turning it. They went inside. The room was spotless and there was a human form crouched beside the bed. All of Luce's belongings were packed away in a large trunk. There was no sign of Martin. Zebulon signaled for the castle steward and the guard to stay before following Luce into the dressing room. Curled up in the corner of the room was Martin. The cheery smile was gone as was any sign of the happy-go-lucky assistant.

"Martin" Luce said. Martin looked at Luce and then looked at Zebulon. He looked scared, but in control.

"I need to get you to answer some questions," Zebulon said as he crouched down to be more level to Martin.

"They will kill me," Martin said

"I will grant you asylum for your answers." Zebulon said, "Everyone who would kill you will be removed from the kingdom. And Luce will protect you until we know you are safe."

"Jarlan, Atius, and Gaius," Martin said, "I found out the plan to kill you and they told me I could not tell you or they would kill me as well. They poisoned your meal. But you did not die. They sent assassins and you did not die. Gaius sent the Reeze, but you survived. He thought I had told you about the plan and that you were surviving because you knew what they were doing. When they forced me to drink the poisoned wine I did not think I would wake up."

"Either they did not know what the poison did," Luce said, "or they did it simply to stop you from telling anyone while they tried to figure out a new plan."

"What was their whole plan?" Zebulon asked.

"Just to kill you and bring your sister back to take the throne," Martin said, "that was all I heard."

"Okay, thank you," Zebulon said as he slowly got to his feet. He left the dressing room. The castle steward and the guard were waiting for him.

"Let us go to the throne room and deal with the Jarlan, Atius, and Gaius," Zebulon said. The steward nodded. Zebulon went passed them and out of the room. Out in the hallway was Lord Menawa and one of the guard.

"I tried to keep him to the throne room, but he said he had to see you," the guard said.

"It is all right." Zebulon waved off the guard, "Say what you have to say as we walk."

Everyone followed, except Lord Menawa who fell into step.

"The man from Jagel has corrupted my daughter." Lord Menawa said, "I want him to pay for the damages he has done."

"After I deal with my first issue, that will be my second." Zebulon said, "Come to throne room."

"Yes, Your Majesty," Lord Menawa said before falling a back a step.

The group reached the throne room. Zebulon went to his throne, but did not sit down. He could see that there was something wrong with the throne and he did not want to die at this point. He turned back to the group gathered in the throne room.

Two guards and the steward were separating Jarlan, Atius, and Gaius from everyone else and in front of the dais. Everyone else moved back as if to distance themselves from the three diplomats. Zebulon noticed that Jarlan had a bruise on his face in place where Dard had hit the man on the balcony.

"You are guests in this kingdom." Zebulon said to the three, "I welcomed you on the basis that you were here to so that our kingdoms could sign a treaty of peace. By your behaviour, I would say that peace was the last thing you truly wanted."

"We have done nothing by wait for you as you waste our time," Gaius said.

"Then would you like to explain the wine poisoned by moa root that just about killed a member of my court," Zebulon said. He took out the vial of the moa root tea and held it out.

"I have never seen it before," Gaius said.

"Then why was it found in your room?" Zebulon asked, "The tea was found in your room, the instructions were found in Jarlan's room, and the kettle it was made in was found in Atius's room. The poison was in the wine that was meant for supper. If the bottle had not been tested beforehand, more people would have in danger. I cannot allow such things to happen in my kingdom. Treaties with your kingdoms are not worth the trouble you are causing."

"That tea, along with the rest of it, could easily be placed there by someone else." Jarlan said, "We are just easy targets."

"Your Majesty," Garrick said.

"Yes, Garrick," Zebulon said.

"I finished my investigation into the murder of Martin," Garrick said.

"What are the results of that investigation?" Zebulon asked.

"Gaius, Jarlan, and Atius were seen carrying Martin's body through the hallway early on the morning it was found by the kitchen door." Garrick said, "The poison used was found nearby. The poison is made from a moss that only grows in Lithimin."

"You are the ones who lost Martin's body," Gaius said.

"Martin is not lost." Zebulon said, "He is currently afraid for his life."

"Martin is dead," Gaius said.

"The moss creates a deep sleep, but does not kill the person." Garrick said, "I have not been looking for his body, but for him. He is likely to be awake by now."

"All treaties are with your kingdoms are off." Zebulon said, "I have a big enough army that none of you dare attack. My father taught me how to command an army and that is what I will do just that if I get word of any attempts at attack. You will go back to your kingdoms and tell your kings that there will be no trading between you and Proster. As of now, trade with Lithimin, Sendal and Grackle is illegal."

It was quiet in the throne room.

"You three will be escorted home this evening," Zebulon said, "because if I see you here again I will have you executed."

"We will pack our stuff and go," Jarlan said.

"Take them away," Zebulon ordered the guards. The three diplomats were dragged off by the guards.

The people left in the court stayed where they were because Zebulon had not moved.

"Myles," Zebulon called. Myles was quickly found in the crowd and pushed forward.

"Yes, Your Majesty," Myles bowed.

"Lord Menawa has brought up an issue he has with you," Zebulon said.

"What is it, Your Majesty?" Myles asked.

"He demands compensation for corrupting his daughter," Zebulon said.

Myles looked nervous and swallowed.

"Your Majesty," Lord Menawa's daughter stepped forward.

"Yes," Zebulon said looking at her.

"I am my own person, why should I not be allowed to make my own choices?" Lord Menawa's daughter asked.

"Your father is responsible for you until you are married," Zebulon said, "as such he has the right to claim compensation. Unless Myles is willing to marry you, he owes your father."

"That is nonsense," Lord Menawa's daughter said.

"I will marry her," Myles piped up.

"Do you accept this, Lord Menawa?" Zebulon asked.

"It sounds like I do not have any other choice," Lord Menawa answered.

"Myles, I would suggest you send a message back to Jagel explaining the situation." Zebulon said, "Lord Menawa, make certain that your daughter is at the church this evening. Garrick, I put you in charge of Myles. Make sure that he gets to the church. Herwin, go explain to the priest what is happening."

"Yes, Your Majesty," Herwin said.

"Everyone else is dismissed," Zebulon said.

Slowly everyone headed out of the throne room. The castle steward did no leave, but stayed until it was only him and Zebulon left.

"Is there anything else you need?" the steward asked.

"My throne has been bobby trapped." Zebulon answered, "Perhaps you can help me deal with it in a way that neither of us gets hurt."

"I will do my best," the steward said coming forward.

They managed to figure it out before the steward went off to his own work and Zebulon went into his office. Zebulon checked the office over, but did not find any more traps. He sat down at the desk to sign the treaty and do other paperwork.

It was late evening when there came a knock at the door to Zebulon's office.

"Come in," Zebulon called. The door opened and the castle steward stepped inside.

"The head cook said that Dard is awake," the steward said.

"Thank you," Zebulon said. The steward left as Zebulon got to his feet. Zebulon headed for the store room. Reaching it, he found Dard sitting on the cot with a glass of water in his hands. No one else was in sight.

"How are you doing?" Zebulon asked.

"Thirsty and tired." Dard answered, "My father told me what happened. I remember having the drink, and then everything after that is just the memory of pain. Did you find the person with the moa root?"

"The three conspirators, Jarlan, Atius, and Gaius, had the moa root and the instructions on how to make it into tea." Zebulon said, "Jarlan also had a bruise on his face from you hitting him after his attempt to throw Thalia off the balcony. I have sent them back to their own kingdoms with the threat of war if they try anything."

"What do you think is going to happen?" Dard asked.

"I am hoping that none of the kingdoms are stupid enough to start a war." Zebulon said, "Though if they do, Wodend has agreed to be our ally."

"And Jagel?" Dard asked.

"Myles wrote a letter to the king." Zebulon answered, "Hopefully, we will get an answer back in a few days."

"Why not send Myles back?" Dard asked.

"Because he could not afford to compensate Lord Menawa for corrupting his daughter." Zebulon said, "They are married now and I doubt that Myles will ever see Jagel again."

"Anything else happen while I was out?" Dard asked.

"Proster has a treaty with Wodend." Zebulon answered, "I had a long and interesting talk with Luce. He was the one who had the antidote that cured you. He asked that you quit trying to follow him around, but with the three diplomats dealt with I do not think that is a worry anymore. Martin is not dead, but was just given a sleeping potion. They thought it was poison when they gave it to him, but really it made him appear dead. Luce has been hiding him and I offered him asylum. He told me that Jarlan, Atius, and Gaius were planning on killing me and that he had been poisoned because they were worried he would tell me about it."

"Well, that is most of the problems of the kingdom solved right there," Dard said.

"But not all of them." Zebulon said, "I will be holding court whenever the woman shows up about the death of her daughter."

"Tomorrow, I think it was," Dard said.

"Good," Zebulon said, "you get some rest. I cannot give you a title if you are not there to receive it."

"I will be there," Dard said.

"Good night," Zebulon said.

"Good night," Dard replied.

Zebulon left the store room. He went up to his bed chamber. He checked it over for traps, but there was not any. He stripped and climbed into bed.

Zebulon stared at his breakfast. It was not that he was not hungry, but that he really did not feel like eating. He had eaten a few bites to avoid people looking at him with concern. The dining room was empty except for a few people at a couple tables. Zebulon had seen Dard up and around, which was good. Dard did not even look like he had been poisoned. Zebulon had not seen Herwin or Garrick yet. He had expected them to find him and tell him how wrong he was for kicking the diplomats out without some guarantee that they would not attack Proster. There was no treaty that could do that after what those three had done. So, Zebulon's morning had been quiet and he had enjoyed it. He expected to hold court later in the morning, but part of that had to wait until the lower court started.

Zebulon pushed his bowl away and stood up. No one else moved as he walked across the room and out the door. He headed to the main door to throne room. Zebulon reached the main hall when he came across Herwin, Garrick and Loic standing in the middle of the hallway and talking quietly.

"Is there something wrong?" Zebulon asked. The men looked at him.

"It is not a serious matter for the kingdom, Your Majesty." Loic answered, "I was just asking Herwin and Garrick for advice on a personal matter."

"You all seem to have a problem coming up with a solution," Zebulon said.

"It is not an easy matter to solve." Garrick replied, "Lady Clarinda has stumbled into some trouble."

"What happened?" Zebulon asked.

"Lord Breton's young son, Blaine, has been having a relationship with Clarinda." Loic said, "She broke it off when I found out and told her that it was inappropriate, but he claims that it is over when he says, not her. Nothing seems to deter him. He claims that she has to marry him no matter what anyone else says. I have talked to him and even threatened him, but he believes himself immune to being harmed. Lord Breton is too sick to do anything about it. Lady Breton refuses to do anything about, except perhaps plan the wedding. Angus is encouraging the whole matter. I feel like I am at my wits end trying to figure out a solution."

"We have suggested locking him in the dungeon, but nothing he has done is illegal." Garrick said, "I cannot think of any way out of it."

"Have Clarinda become engaged to someone else." Zebulon said, "If she is already taken then Blaine cannot demand she marry him."

"I cannot find anyone who would be willing to stand up to Blaine," Loic said.

A guard came down the hallway.

"Sire, and sirs," the guard bowed when he reached them, "There is a woman here that is begging for an audience. I told her that the lower court will start in an hour, but she says that it is not a matter for the lower court. She claims that Dard told her to demand the higher court. What should I do with her?"

"Ask her to wait." Zebulon answered, "The royal court will be meeting shortly and she will be allowed in then."

"Yes, Sire," the guard bowed and again before leaving.

"Who is she?" Herwin asked.

"Dard told me about her," Zebulon answered, "and I have been expecting her. Loic and Garrick, go get Lord Breton and family for court. I expect them all to be there."

"Yes, Your Majesty," Garrick said. He and Loic bowed before going off.

"What are you planning on doing?" Herwin asked.

"To hear her case out." Zebulon answered, "There is nothing else that I had planned, except maybe punishing those that did wrong."

"And you know who are the ones that need punishing?" Herwin asked.

"I am familiar with the case," Zebulon answered.

"Perhaps you can help Loic and Clarinda while there is court." Herwin said, "You are the king and people are not likely to go up against you."

"I am going to guess that you are suggesting that I marry Clarinda," Zebulon said.

"She needs the help," Herwin said, "and the kingdom needs a queen. You refused all the portraits and have angered the kings. Jagel is likely to not be as upset, but I still doubt that they want to have a treaty since you will not be sending a male back to their country."

"There will be no such announcements at court today," Zebulon said as he turned away from Herwin. Zebulon headed for his office.

Upon entering, Zebulon found Dard sitting there. Zebulon closed the door and down in his own chair.

"I did not have time to tell you what I found before I was poisoned," Dard said, "and afterward things got a little busy."

"So, you are here to tell me," Zebulon said.

"Angus is using Orestes as an accomplice when he goes out to terrorize the people." Dard said, "The point being that the guards catch Orestes and he gets in trouble while Angus gets off free. The only reason they have not had to use the system is because the guards have not been there at the right time to catch them in the act. There are a lot of stories from the people afterward who can identify Angus, but the guards are never there at the time. So, neither of them have gotten caught. The stories do say that Orestes does not do anywhere near as much damage as Angus. He also does not take the same sense of glee out of doing it."

"And apparently Angus's younger brother is as bad as he is." Zebulon said, "Lady Clarinda was having a relationship with Blaine and now he will not let her break up with him. Loic is at his wits end trying to find a solution, because Blaine believes himself as immune to punishment as Angus is."

"Your court is out of control," Dard said.

"I hope that punishing Angus will have an effect on Blaine." Zebulon said, "If he believes that he will be punished perhaps he will stop."

"And if he does not stop?" Dard said, "What will Loic do about his daughter?"

"Herwin suggested that I marry Lady Clarinda," Zebulon said.

"That might not be a bad match." Dard said, "She is from Proster, which was important to you. She knows the current politics. And she is not bad looking, if you do not mind pink. You need someone who can be your queen and produce an heir. You may one day love her, but you do not need to right off. I would suggest that you both discuss the terms of your marriage beforehand so that you both know what you are getting out of the relationship."

"I will consider this if, and only if, Blaine does not let up after Angus is punished," Zebulon said.

"Willingness to consider it is a good start," Dard said.

There was a knock at the door.

"Come in," Zebulon called. The door opened and Luce stepped into the room. He closed the door behind him.

"Both of you know each other," Zebulon said.

"Yes," Dard replied.

"I hope you are doing well," Luce said.

"I am," Dard said, "and I am told it is thanks to you that I am even alive."

"I consider a service to the crown," Luce said.

"And the crown thanks you for it," Zebulon said.

"You are both welcome." Luce said, "I came to stop in and see if you signed the treaty."

"I did," Zebulon said picking up the scroll and offering it to Luce.

"That is wonderful." Luce said, "I hope that we are in for a long, fruitful alliance."

"With the results of last night's events, I might have to call upon Wodend for help with the war," Zebulon said.

"I am sure that support will be provided." Luce said, "That is what allies are for."

"That is what friends are for," Zebulon said as he stood up and held out his hand.

"And hopefully a long friendship," Luce said with a smile. He shook Zebulon's hand.

"You are welcome to do your research any time you are ready," Zebulon said.

"I will do that." Luce said, "I must return to Wodend with the treaty, and then I will be able to start my research. I bid you both goodbye and good luck for things to come."

"Good bye and have a safe journey," Zebulon said.

"Good bye and thank you again," Dard said as he stood up. He and Luce shook hands. Then Luce left the office. He closed the door behind him.

"And now on to the next problem," Zebulon said as he made sure he looked the part of the king.

"You will do fine." Dard said, "I have to be off to get the woman. I told her that I would represent her in court if she needed. She said that she would appreciate that. I will go meet her and wait for your order to come in."

"I will see you in there," Zebulon said.

Dard left the office and closed the door behind him. Zebulon went to the door that led straight into the throne room and opened it. He stepped through and into the throne room. It was empty, except for a guard at the door. Zebulon sat down on the throne and got himself comfortable before nodding to the guard. The guard bowed and left the room.

A few minutes past before the doors were opened and people started coming in. They drifted to either side of the carpet down the middle that led to the dais. Lord and Lady Breton arrived with both Angus and Blaine. Orestes was not that far behind him. Clarinda was there, but she moved to the opposite side from Lord Breton and family. Nasia was also there and as always she seemed to be following Orestes. Several older lords who did not make a habit of coming to court were there. Garrick came in and moved to stand behind the throne. Herwin must have been in charge of the lower court today. Dard did not come in, nor did the woman.

Zebulon waited until everyone arrived and settled in. Then the guard from earlier came in and bowed.

"Yes?" Zebulon asked. The guard straightened up.

"Your Majesty, there is a woman, by the name of Alethea, here asking for an audience." the guard said, "Dard is with her and is willing to represent her."

"Her request is granted," Zebulon said.

"Yes, Your Majesty," the guard bowed before turning to leave. The throne room was quiet as they waited. Less than five minutes passed before Alethea and Dard entered the throne room. They bowed at the doorway.

"You may approach," Zebulon said. Both straightened and moved forward. They stopped at the appropriate distance and bowed again. Dard had stopped a few feet behind the woman. She was dressed in clothes that were too big on her, but they did not have any holes and very few stains. They still looked the rags compared to the people standing around her. She had pulled her hair back in a braid, but it was very messy. Her eyes looked sad and tired, but there was some determination in her frame. The resemblance between her and her daughter was enough that Zebulon had to force himself not to give off any hint that she was familiar and push his feelings on the matter far enough down that they could not bubble up in the middle of this.

"What do you bring before me?" Zebulon asked.

"My daughter was murdered by a member of your court." Alethea answered, "I am here to demand that he be punished for that crime."

"Do you know the identity of the member?" Zebulon asked.

"Him," Alethea said pointing to Angus, "and his friend." She then pointed to Orestes.

"What happened?" Zebulon asked.

"My daughter and I had a stall in the market place where we sold vegetables for our living," Alethea said, "as has been our need since my husband's death. My daughter would step out into the street and call to people going passed in hopes that they would be interested. She did this only on days when there were more people than wagons. Three days ago, we were in the market place at our stall. No wagons had gone passed for hours when she stepped out into the street to try and interest people. She would go back and forth across the road as well as up and down along it. It was getting close to the time that we would pack up and go home, but we still needed a little bit more money to afford bread for our supper. She continued to go into the street and get someone to buy something. Then a carriage came down the street. She was coming back to the stall and out of the street. The carriage was coming too fast for her to get out of the way and the carriage moved in an effort to hit her. Then the wheels rolled over her. The carriage was gone before I could even shout a warning. I went to her and found her to be dead."

"You saw a carriage hit your daughter," Zebulon said, "but how can you be sure that it was those two members of my court?"

"I saw them through the window." Alethea answered, "The curtains were open and I could see their faces as they laughed over what they were doing." Alethea looked like she wanted to start crying, but she held herself together.

"I have the testimonies of others who witnessed the accident," Dard said, "as well as guard who investigated it."

"Bring them forward," Zebulon said. Dard turned and signalled someone through the open door to the throne room. Three men in rags entered and one member of the guard came with them. Alethea stepped back to let them come forward. All bowed when they reached the spot she had just left.

"The first man, is Bancroft," Dard indicated the man in the centre with a washed face, but rags that had been patched more times than there was original material in his clothes, "He was also along the street at the time."

"What is your version of the events that took place?" Zebulon asked.

"I was on my way to deliver some clothes that I had fixed." Bancroft answered, "When a carriage came barreling out of nowhere and slammed into the woman who sells vegetables. She tried to get out of the way, but he went after her. The men inside the carriage were laughing at it all. They knew the carriage had hit her and they laughed about it."

"And who were the men in the carriage?" Zebulon asked. Bancroft looked around the throne room until he saw them.

"Those two," Bancroft pointed to Angus and Orestes.

"Thank you for your testimony," Zebulon said. Bancroft bowed and moved off to one side.

"This is Hyman," Dard said indicating the next man. This man was athletic and tall. His clothes were of a better quality, but his shoes looked like they were coming apart.

"What did you see?' Zebulon asked.

"I was stopped at a stall waiting for a reply to the message I have delivered when there was the sound of wheels on the cobblestones." Hyman said, "I crowded into the stall as the carriage went passed to avoid being hit. I could see the two men inside because the curtains were open. The vegetable seller was trying to get out of the way, but the carriage hit her."

"Did see the driver try to hit her?" Zebulon asked.

"No," Hyman said, "but I was behind the carriage and not in front or to one side."

"Can you identify the men from the carriage?" Zebulon asked.

"Yes," Hyman answered, "it is the two men over there." Hyman pointed to Angus and Orestes.

"Thank you for testifying," Zebulon said. Hyman bowed and moved to stand next to Bancroft.

"And this is Edan," Dard said pointed to the next man. Edan was dressed as one of the merchants from the stalls. His clothes had no holes in them and his face had been washed, but there was still dirt. He carried no extra weight, but was not skinny either.

"What did you see?" Zebulon asked.

"A carriage with the crest on the door came down the street at a fast pace." Egan answered, "Alethea's daughter had been trying to get people's attention and interest by stepping out into the street. She saw the carriage and moved to get out of the way. As she moved to the side of the road the carriage was directed toward her. It slammed into her and she went down. Both wheels on that side then rolled over her. I could clearly see both men in the carriage as they laughed. The carriage continued on at the same pace as before."

"And you can identify the men in the carriage?" Zebulon asked.

"I can." Edan said, "It is the two men over there." Edan answered as he pointed to Angus and Orestes.

"Thank you for your account," Zebulon said. Edan bowed moved to one side. The guard took one step forward and bowed.

"Tell us about your investigation," Zebulon said.

"Yes, Your Majesty." the guard said, "My partner and I were attracted by a disturbance when we were on our patrol. We were just below the market place. We followed the road up and found people were in disarray. Some baskets were in the middle of the road and had been smashed by a wagon. We asked people what had happened and they reported a carriage going through the area at a high speed. We followed the trial of damage and shattered nerves. All the people could describe the carriage with the crest on the door and two men inside laughing. All of them had similar descriptions of the men, which match the two men over there. There were reports of the carriage trying to intentionally run people down, but no one had been struck at that point.

"We followed the path of destruction to the road. We came across other patrols who had also heard the commotion and were following the carriage. Unfortunately, the carriage was going at speed and we were walking. We never caught up to the carriage while it was racing through the market place. However, we did come across Alethea hugging her daughter's corpse. We talked to as many of the people we could in the area about the incident. They all reported the carriage going through and hitting the woman. All were similar to what the court just heard. We got the undertaker to come and take away the body. Alethea was escorted home. Once we had done what we could there, my partner and I continued to follow the damage caused by the carriage. It led us up for a few more blocks before it stopped. The carriage apparently slowed down and had gone off to somewhere else. There were still reports that the carriage was aiming for people, though no one else was killed. There were a few injuries, but nothing severe. We followed the description of the crest to Lord Breton, but had not taken it any farther as of yet."

"Anything else?" Zebulon asked when the guard paused.

"Yes," the guard said, "although it has not been witnessed by a member of the guard, the described suspects have been implicated in numerous incidents that have happened in the market place and the lower part of the city. We had identified them, but it was difficult to get the people who had witnesses the crimes to testify to what they had seen. As such there was nothing we could do about the men. Included in these incidents are the torturing of a beggar, the kidnapping and rape of a girl, the beating of a stall owner, and the burning of another beggar. Though the one man has been involved in many more incidents and more involved in the incidents than the other man."

"Which one has had more involvement?" Zebulon asked.

"Angus Breton." the guard answered, "As stated we have not been able to get the evidence needed to bring it before the court until now."

"Thank you for your report," Zebulon said. The guard bowed and stepped back out of the way.

"Angus and Orestes," Zebulon called. The two of them moved closer to the dais.

"Yes, Your Majesty?" Angus asked.

"What is your defence?" Zebulon asked.

"They are all lying because they believe they can gain something from making me look bad." Angus answered, "They saw a crest on the side of the carriage and thought it was mine because I had been through that area the day before. They all claim that the carriage was going fast, but they saw the crest and the people inside. The speed would have prevented them from getting a good view. Also if I were to run rampant through the market place, I would not be stupid enough to leave the curtains open. So, I say they are all lying because somewhere in their minds they believe that they will gain something from this."

"And what is your defence, Orestes?" Zebulon asked. Orestes looked at Angus for half a moment. Angus glared back.

"They must have been confused." Orestes answered as he looked up at Zebulon, "The carriage was going at speed and they did not see things clearly. They substituted the carriage they had seen the day before with the one that sped by that day."

"Is that your whole defence?" Zebulon asked, "Personal gain and confusion?"

"Yes, Your Majesty," Angus answered.

"Dard?" Zebulon said.

"I can tell everyone that these people do not gain anything from being here today." Dard said, "All they get is the loss of valuable time from their days. They could be out making money to feed themselves tonight. Alethea has lost something very precious and gains nothing unless justice is done here in this court. As for confusion, I might believe it if the same information was not repeated by each person in different ways. They all saw the same crest and they all saw the same two men inside the carriage. They all gave the event from different perspectives, giving creditability to their stories. As for the foolishness of leaving the curtains open, I would assume that had to do with enjoying the destruction and believing to be immune from punishment."

"Anyone else have something to say about this case?" Zebulon addressed the whole room and then waited to see if anyone had something they wanted to say. The throne room was silent. Zebulon waited a minute longer.

"Then I will make a ruling in this case and the results will be final," Zebulon said. He paused again, but the throne room remained silent.

"I declare Angus and Orestes guilty of the murder by carriage of Alethea's daughter," Zebulon said, "as such Alethea will be compensated for the loss of her daughter through the Breton estate of twenty gold pieces a month for the rest of her life. As for Angus and Orestes, they are to be hung until dead in the court yard by supper time. Is there any objection to this pronouncement?"

The court room was silent in response. Zebulon let the silence linger a little longer. He looked over at Lord Breton and his wife. Blaine was giving a smirk that suggested he thought his brother was stupid to get caught. Alethea was waiting for the moment when there was closure to this horrible time, while being scared that someone would say something and she would forced to live this moment for a long time. Everyone else was waiting with looks that suggested they did not want to object to the king.

"I object," the voice was quiet, but definitely female. The people around Nasia looked at her and moved away from her as if she suddenly had the plague.

"Come forward," Zebulon said. Nasia took a deep breath and moved forward.

"Why do you object?" Zebulon asked.

"I love him," Nasia pointed to Orestes. She appeared to be close to tears.

"Then Orestes is given a reprieve as long as he swears that not to be involved in such behaviour ever again," Zebulon said.

"I swear that I will never be involved in such behaviour as long as I live," Orestes said.

"Then you will live with these conditions." Zebulon said, "You and Nasia will be married before the day is out. After that you will be spend your time looking after Lord Breton, since he is failing in health and needs a man in his house to take care of things."

Blaine's smirk dimmed, but did not fade away.

"I accept those conditions," Orestes said.

Two guards had come into the throne room and were headed towards Angus. Angus noticed them and followed their progress towards him.

"Angus Breton, you are under arrest and will be executed this day," Zebulon said.

Angus dropped a knife from his sleeve into his hand and grabbed Alethea, who was closest. He placed the knife at her neck.

"Come any closer and I will kill her," Angus told the guards as they were coming towards him. He has turned his back on Zebulon to focus on the guards. The guards stopped and appeared to be unsure of how to proceed. The whole court gasped and backed away from Angus as if to avoid being in danger.

Zebulon slowly got up, but everyone's attention was on Angus.

"Make a path between me and the door," Angus demanded. Zebulon went up behind Angus. He clamped one hand around Angus's windpipe and the other hand around Angus's wrist. Alethea used the opportunity to kick Angus in the knee and get away. Angus lost his grip on the knife before reaching up and trying to remove Zebulon's hand. Zebulon cut off the air flow and slowly Angus lost consciousness. Once he was out, Zebulon let go and Angus slid to the floor. The guards rushed forward and grabbed Angus. They hauled him out of there.

Zebulon turned and went back to his throne. He sat down and looked over the stunned crowd.

"Court is dismissed for today," Zebulon announced. Slowly people left as they murmured to each other. Dard escorted Alethea and the witnesses out. Blaine moved to where he could follow Clarinda out. She did not look happy about it. Finally everyone had left the throne room, except Zebulon and Garrick. Garrick still stood in his place as advisor.

"Is there something you want to say?" Zebulon asked.

"Sometimes you do things that remind me that you are your father's son," Garrick answered, "and sometimes you do things that your father would not have bothered with. Before this I kept wondering which one was the better way to rule. That showed me that both work well together."

Garrick moved to the area in front of the dais. He bowed and then left the throne room. Zebulon sat there until Garrick was gone. Then he got down and went into his office.

Zebulon sat in the chair beside the fireplace reading a book about the saints while he waited to be called for lunch.

Finally a knock came at the door.

"Come in," Zebulon called as he put his finger in the book before closing it to look at the door. The door opened and the castle steward stepped inside.

"Lunch is in the dining room, sire," the castle steward said.

"Thank you," Zebulon said.

"Also the guards have constructed a make shift gallows in the court yard for when you are ready to execute Angus," the steward said, "and you are invited to the wedding that will take place after that."

"Thank you," Zebulon said.

The castle steward bowed and then left the office. Zebulon found a bookmark before heading to the dining room.

After lunch, Zebulon went out to the balcony. This time it was empty. He went to the edge and looked down into the court yard. The gallows had been set up with a rope and a pile of crates at one of the flag poles in the wall.

"Ready for your first execution as king?" Dard asked.

"No." Zebulon answered, "I do not want to kill him, but he took her life away. That moment on that street, he destroyed the one thing in life I truly loved. I cannot get that back no matter what I do. For that he deserves to die."

"What if someone had objected to him dying?" Dard asked, "Would you have gone back on executing him?"

"I would have listened to what they had to say," Zebulon said, "And then I would have figured out a way around that. Angus was going to pay for what he did and this was the only way fitting. His life as payment for hers."

"I am sure that there are others that feel the same way," Dard said, "but I think you also made your court realize that you were not the lazy son of a great man. That you yourself are a great man."

"Maybe you can remind them when one of them decides that peasants do not have a right to live their own lives." Zebulon said, "Angus is not the only noble that does not know how to treat the people of this kingdom."

"You will find them and deal with them." Dard said, "Hopefully before any of them get as bad as Angus."

"I need to keep an ear out for what the people need," Zebulon said, "especially since they are the ones that matter."

"Does that mean I do not get my title?" Dard asked.

"No, that means I am going to read the reports from the guards who patrol the city," Zebulon said, "and visit the market place regularly."

"Those are good ways to keep in touch with the people," Dard said.

"Speaking of your title, how is Thalia?" Zebulon asked.

"She is fine." Dard said, "We have a lot more to talk about now. She still will not let me in because she has not confirmed who I am."

"Tell her the truth," Zebulon said.

"I am the head cook's son, please do not walk away, I can explain." Dard said, "That does not sound good, even for someone as liberal minded as she is."

"How about I am the head cook's son, but do to my help, King Zebulon has seen it fit to get me this title so that I may be a proper member of his court?" Zebulon asked.

"You give me a title and I will use it," Dard said.

"It is coming," Zebulon said.

"Your Majesty," the castle steward said after clearing his throat, "They want to know if you are ready for them to start the execution. People have been gathering in the court yard since lunch and most of them are here already."

"Go ahead." Zebulon said, "Tell them to give me a signal when they are ready and I will give the order."

"Yes, Sire," the castle steward said, bowed, and went back inside.

Zebulon and Dard turned their attention to the court yard below them. As the castle steward said the crowd had gathered and were waiting for the execution. Lord Breton and his wife had been provided with chairs. Blaine, Orestes, and Nasia were nearby them. The rest of the crowd were directed by the guards as to how far to keep back and the rest of it. The executioner made sure that everything was ready. He flashed a sign up to Zebulon.

"Bring out the prisoner," Zebulon called. There was a drum roll and Angus was brought out from wherever they had been keeping him. He was in chains and looked like he had been in a few fights that he lost. Two guards on either side of him made sure that he stayed in the pathway they had laid out. They marched him to where the noose was waiting. Once there, Angus was set up on the top crate and the noose was placed around his neck. When they were finished they looked up at Zebulon.

"Angus Breton, you are being hung for the murder of Alethea's daughter." Zebulon called down, "Do you have any last words?"

"No," Angus called back.

"Let it be done," Zebulon called.

The executioner kicked the bottom crate out from under the pile and the rest fell over causing Angus to fall quickly to the end of the rope. His neck snapped and he hung limply from the rope. The executor cut him down and he was put into a coffin. The undertaker took the coffin away in a wagon.

"And that is the last of Angus Breton," Zebulon said. The crown below started to drift off. Zebulon and Dard headed back inside.

They headed down to the main entrance of the castle. Outside were several carriages, one was Lord Breton's carriage and one was the royal carriage. Lord Breton and family were getting into the one. Zebulon got into the other, along with Dard. Thalia climbed in after him along with one of the ladies who was always around her. They were quiet as the carriage started.

The carriage took them to the church where they were dropped off at the steps. Dard got down first and helped Thalia and the other lady out. Zebulon climbed out on his own. He followed the crowd going into the church and took the pew that was second from the front, which was reserved for royalty. Everyone else drifted in and found seats. Lord and Lady Breton sat down in the front pew. The priest and Orestes went to the front of the church and waited there.

Finally everyone had arrived and was seated. The organist started playing the wedding march and everyone stood up. The bride came down the aisle in a dress that she must have borrowed and quickly adjusted, but still looked beautiful in. She went to the front of the church and the priest started into the ceremony. He gave a long and flowery description of what love was and what it meant. He talked about Saint Lang being the saint of love because Saint Lang had found love so beautiful and wanted everyone in the world to feel it at least once in their life. Saint Lang was known for manipulating people into finding their beloveds. The priest asked both Nasia and Orestes if they agreed to the conditions that were part of marriage. They both agreed. He declared them married and said a blessing over them.

The bride and groom stopped to get Lord and Lady Breton on their way out of the church. Once they had left, the rest of the crowd drifted out talking about how sweet the ceremony had been. Zebulon waited until most of them had left before getting up. He went out to his carriage, which was waiting for him. Dard was the only one inside.

"Did we lose the other two?" Zebulon asked.

"They were invited to celebrate the wedding with some other friends." Dard answered, "So, they ditched us. I was not invited and she did not ask if I could come, so I am going back to the castle with you."

"I hope someday you will get to go with her." Zebulon said, "It is better than both of us going back to the castle lonely."

"You can marry Clarinda and then you will not be lonely," Dard said.

"Clarinda is not a cure for loneliness." Zebulon said, "She has her own life and would never want to be tied down just because she was married. The only thing I would get out of marrying her is a child and that is only if I put it in as part of getting married. That is hardly a way to stop being lonely."

"Well, it was a thought anyway," Dard said.

They did not speak for the rest of the way back to the castle. When the carriage stopped outside the door, they both got out and went inside.

ZEBULON IS TO GET MARRIED, BUT DARD GETS HIS HAPPILY EVER AFTER

Dard went off while Zebulon headed for the kitchen. Once there he poured two mugs of ale and took them out the kitchen door to the court yard. Everyone had cleared out and the only people left were the guards and the servants cleaning up. Zebulon went into the alcove beside the kitchen door. There was no one in there. Zebulon set both mugs in the middle before sitting down against one wall. He picked up his mug, but did not drink any of it. He closed his eyes.

"Saint Lang," Zebulon said.

"Have you found your purpose?" Saint Lang asked.

"To be a king for the people of this kingdom," Zebulon answered as he opened his eyes. The man who sat there was the man from the story, not the old beggar. He had picked up the mug and was taking a sip.

"You certainly have been setting up marriages." Saint Lang said, "I have not seen so much matchmaking since the love potion incident. Two in two days, and both good matches."

"I am not worried about whether they are good matches as much as getting them married." Zebulon said, "I had no other choice with Myles, for some reason he could not pay the money."

"But you could have killed Orestes rather than have him marry Nasia." Saint Lang said, "That would have destroyed her, but most people would have ignored her. After love is not important."

"Love is very important." Zebulon said, "Without it there is nothing worth doing. I am just barely learning how to live without love and I never really was loved. I did all the loving and it was from a distance."

"Perhaps you could fall in love again, if you give yourself a chance," Saint Lang said.

"I am part dwarf." Zebulon said, "My father told that as part dwarf it was likely that I would find one person who was my true love and never find love other than that."

"Then why wait so long to go down and talk to her?" Saint Lang said, "You might have saved her life if you had."

"I was never sure what to say, or how to say it." Zebulon said, "She was so beautiful, I felt that anything I said would sound foolish."

"Love is never foolish if it is true," Saint Lang said.

"But it felt like it," Zebulon said.

"If you are part dwarf, you are also half human." Saint Lang said, "Humans can have multiple loves in their lives. So, you may have had a true love, but that does not preclude all other loves from your life."

"No," Zebulon said, "but the feeling of true love cannot be matched."

"So, you have to settle for second best." Saint Lang said, "There is a saying that hesitation is the biggest cause of missed opportunities. The love that develops over time can be just as powerful as true love."

"I said that I would think about marrying Clarinda if Blaine keeps bothering her," Zebulon said as he set his empty mug on the ground beside him.

"Are you looking for a way out?" Saint Lang asked.

"I wanted the woman I married to be my choice, not something that was pushed on to me." Zebulon said, "I did not want the other people to pick the person out."

"Your father accepted the woman who was shown to him," Saint Lang said.

"Except that was true love," Zebulon said.

"Then you had your chance to choose." Saint Lang said, "Now is your time for acceptance."

Zebulon leaned his head back against the wall. The frustration on his face switched to tiredness.

"So, I get a second choice of a woman who does not love me, even if she wants to be queen, because I could not manage to talk to my true love," Zebulon said, "and this was all decided by someone else. Is there any good points to all this?"

"There are always good points." Saint Lang said, "You just have to look for them."

Zebulon closed his eyes to prevent himself from getting frustrated again.

"Name one?" Zebulon said.

"Your son," Saint Lang's voice drifted off.

An image appeared in Zebulon's head. It was a small boy of about six. *The boy was running around the garden with one of the dogs from the kitchen chasing him. Clarinda was sitting on one of the benches watching. Dard and Thalia were standing nearby. In Dard's arms was a bundle of pink blankets. He was smiling and everyone's attention went to the boy as he started walking along the low wall around one area of the garden. The boy was laughing and smiling as he fell off the wall. He got back on and came back the way he had gone. He reached the end this time without falling. He ran up to Zebulon for congratulations. Then the boy was off again. He started hoping over flower pots.*

Zebulon drifted off to sleep with a smile on his face.

Zebulon sat in his office and stared at the pile of paperwork that had been left there from the previous day. He had woken up this morning in the alcove with the memory of talking to Saint Lang and the image of the boy. Zebulon had managed to get to his room without meeting up with anyone who would ask him where he had been. He had changed and come down to his office.

The castle steward had brought in breakfast, so Zebulon had eaten. Now the pile of paperwork was the only thing he had to do. And he really did not want to deal with it. Zebulon stared at it for several minutes before getting to his feet. It could wait a couple more hours, there was no rush on any of it, and if there had been a rush someone would be here telling him about it.

Zebulon left his office and went up the stairs to the tower. He got to the top and found it empty as usual. He went to the window and looked out. The clouds had come over the sky, but the rain had not started to fall yet. It would likely do so later. Zebulon took out the spyglass he kept in his pocket. He searched the market place as he always did. Down there, business was as usual, but Alethea was not there and her daughter was definitely not there. Zebulon missed watching the woman as she tried to sell vegetables. He missed coming up here and spending the time by himself.

Zebulon looked over the rest of the town with the spyglass, but there was nothing else of interest going on. He closed the spyglass and put it away. There was nothing up here for him anymore. Everything worth coming up here for was dead. Zebulon headed back down the stairs, but at a slower pace than he went up. There was no rush for anything right now. He had to face the rest of the world and deal with the problems that waited there for him. The woman of his dreams could not hold that reality at bay.

There was nothing but paperwork in the office, so Zebulon did not go in there. This time he headed out to the court yard. Out there he found several guards training, as well as some of the noble ladies watching. Clarinda was sitting there as well, but it did not seem she was there for the spectacle. She appeared to feel safer in a crowd than by herself. Zebulon looked around, but did not see Blaine anywhere in the court yard. Clarinda must have gotten away from him for the morning.

Zebulon watched the guard's practice. They were very good, but they had been trained by Loic and the rest of the warriors that had come with Proster from Grackle. Zebulon had not been trained in the use of any weapon that they were fighting with.

Loic was standing by the side of the fight making sure that they were doing everything correctly and were not doing serious damage to each other. Loic noticed Zebulon and moved to the space beside him.

"What do we owe the honour?" Loic asked.

"Restlessness." Zebulon answered, "I have plenty of other things that I should do, but am having trouble sitting still to do them. How is your problem?"

"It is not resolved itself." Loic answered, "He seems to think he is more immune than Angus, which at the moment is true since he has done nothing illegal. Perhaps to get rid of your restless energy you would like to enter the ring." Loic pointed down to the circles drawn on the cobblestones of the court yard of which were used for practicing.

"I have no proficiency with any of the weapons." Zebulon said, "I know the basics of a sword and spear, but the rest are unknown to me."

"Then we can start with a sword." Loic said, "You can learn the rest as we go."

"Very well." Zebulon said, "Since I have nothing better to do."

"I will go find us some swords," Loic said before going off.

Zebulon took off his coat and set it on a crate near the circle. He adjusted the rest of his clothing so that none of it would hamper him in the fight. When he was finished, Loic arrived back with two training swords. They had guards over them to protect the opponents from each other. Zebulon took one and the two of them stepped into the circle.

Loic took his stance and Zebulon took a similar one opposite him. Loic swung his sword and Zebulon made a clumsy block. Loic moved his sword to strike again and Zebulon swung at Loic's middle. Loic blocked the swing and shoved the sword aside. Zebulon got control of his sword back and was able to block Loic's swing, but it was close to slipping through. Zebulon shoved Loic's sword away and tried to swing. Loic attacked before Zebulon could finish the follow through. The only thing that stopped Loic's attack was that Zebulon stepped on his toe.

Both of them stepped back. They circled each other for a moment. Loic swung at Zebulon's middle. Zebulon brought his sword up and blocked it. Loic pulled his sword away and swung at the other side. Zebulon blocked it. Loic pulled back again and did an overhand swing. Zebulon blocked that swing as well. He knocked Loic's sword aside and thrust his sword toward Loic's stomach. Loic moved to one side and the sword missed him. Loic brought his sword up to strike Zebulon, but was met with Zebulon's sword going down. The swords clashed and they were forced back.

They circled each other again. Zebulon noticed that their fight had brought the rest of the fights to a standstill as everyone stopped to watch them. The noble ladies were also watching the fight. A few people from other parts of the court yard had also gathered to watch.

Loic charged at Zebulon. Zebulon moved out of the way of the charge, but his foot was still there when Loic reached that point and Loic went down. He came close to the edge of the circle. He stopped himself and pulled back. Loic got to his feet and faced Zebulon again. They circled each other again. Loic swung at Zebulon's stomach again. Zebulon brought up his sword to block it and then shoved it away from him before swinging his own sword at Loic's middle. Loic managed to block the sword, but once again Zebulon got too close and stepped on Loic's foot. It was the same foot and Loic pulled his foot up. Zebulon stumbled off it.

They were back to circling each other. This time, Loic was limping a little. Loic charged again, this time he changed directions when Zebulon tried to move. Zebulon stopped and waited until Loic was close to him. Then Zebulon ducked and went up under Loic's sword arm to smash into his stomach. Loic fell backwards on to the cobblestone. Zebulon waited until Loic got up. Loic was starting to breath heavy as they circled each other this time. Loic swung his sword at Zebulon's chest. Zebulon blocked and swung at Loic. Loic blocked and parried. Zebulon blocked and shoved the sword away to smack into Loic's shoulder with his own. Loic exhaled sharply, but did not fall. He brought his sword back into the battle with a swing at Zebulon's head. Zebulon ducked it and moved away from Loic. Loic swung at him again when Zebulon popped back up. Zebulon blocked the swing and brought it down along the other blade. Loic pulled away and swung at Zebulon's wrist. Zebulon pulled his hand out of the way just in time for Loic to miss. The swing took Loic farther than he wanted and Zebulon had his sword back up to strike before Loic could bring his up to block. Zebulon caught Loic's shoulder, but the sword bounced off with the guard on it.

Both men stepped back and circled each other again. This time Loic went around a few more times as he tried to catch his breath. Zebulon found that he was also breathing harder as he went around. Loic stepped up and swung at Zebulon's stomach. Zebulon blocked and then swung at Loic's chest. Loic blocked it and when he swung he also went higher. Zebulon was able to block it and then swing again. Loic blocked it and thrust at

Zebulon. Zebulon blocked it by sending Loic forward. When Loic was in the right position, Zebulon hit him on the hip as he went passed. Loic fell to the ground and this time the sword flying out of his hand. The sword slid across the cobblestones until it stopped outside the circle. Zebulon put the point of the sword to Loic's throat.

"I give," Loic gasped out. Zebulon backed off. He dropped his own sword and then put his hands on his knees as he tried to catch his breath. Loic stayed on the ground a few minutes more before moving to a sitting position.

"You do not have proficiency with a sword," Loic said, "but I would never want to face you in a brawl."

"My father never considered bare hand fighting to be worth anything." Zebulon said, "That was my one form of rebellion to all his rules, was learning bare knuckle fighting. It has worked well so far. Perhaps one day you can teach me the proper way to use a sword."

"It would be my honour," Loic said as he held his hand out. Zebulon took it and helped Loic to his feet. Loic picked up the swords and headed off to put them away. The spectators drifted back to what they had been doing. There was some whispering about the fight, but none of them had been close enough to hear the conversation.

Zebulon went back to where his coat was. Rather than pick it up, he sat down on the crate and looked around. Everything appeared to be the same as before. The guards were fighting and the ladies were watching. But something was wrong. Zebulon went over the scene again. The guards were the same ones as before and there was no one new. The ladies were seated and watching the fights. Zebulon's eyes went back over the group of ladies a third time. Clarinda was gone. Zebulon looked around the court yard. He saw Blaine dragging Clarinda by the arm away from the fights and toward the gateways.

Zebulon stood up and started after them. He could not run without attracting everyone's attention, but he could move at a fast walk without anyone looking at him. He did not reach them before Blaine had managed to drag Clarinda out of the gate, so when Zebulon stepped out he had to look around. He saw them headed to the left and the direction of the house Lord Breton kept in the city. Zebulon continued after them. Blaine was so busy dragging Clarinda and Clarinda was so busy trying to get her arm away from him that they did not notice him.

Zebulon caught up to them when they reached the alley way. He grabbed Blaine and smashed him back first into the wall of the alley way. Clarinda gasped and fell back away from them. Since her arm was now free, Clarinda got up and ran back towards the gate to the court yard.

Zebulon stared down Blaine. Blaine was still young enough that he was not taller than Zebulon. Blaine's face slowly drained of colour as Zebulon's eyes filled with angry.

"You touch her again and I will rip you into pieces so small that your mother will not recognize you," Zebulon's voice was a growl, "Do you understand me?"

"Y-y-y-es," Blaine stuttered. His eyes were filled with fear and his bladder let go.

"Go home to your mother," Zebulon commanded before letting Blaine go. Blaine barely stopped himself from falling to the ground. He took off at a run and did not even look back when he got to the end of the alley way.

Zebulon took a deep breath and let go of the anger that had filled him. He straightened his clothing and dusted himself off. Then Zebulon headed back to the court yard. Inside he looked around, but did not see Clarinda at all. Everyone was still doing what they had been doing when he left.

Zebulon went to his coat and picked it up off the crate before going into the castle. He found the castle steward in the entrance way talking to one of the guards in front of the throne room. He waited until the castle steward was finished.

"Yes, Sire?" the castle steward asked once he was finished talking to the guard.

"Could I get a bath drawn?" Zebulon asked.

"Right away, Your Majesty," the castle steward answered, "Anything else?"

"Not at this time," Zebulon answered. The steward bowed and then went off to fill Zebulon's request. Zebulon made his way to his bed chambers at a much slower pace. By the time he got there the tub was half full. He waited until it had been filled before kicking everyone out, locking the door, and then going for his bath.

Being clean and dressed in a fresh outfit, Zebulon ate lunch in the dining room before going to his office. He sat down at the desk and looked at the pile of paperwork. It did not look quite so bad now. He started with the top one.

Zebulon was half way through the stack when there came a knock at the door.

"Come in," Zebulon called. The door opened and the castle steward stood there.

"Lady Clarinda would like to be granted an audience," the castle steward said from the doorway.

"Send her in," Zebulon said. The steward bowed and took a step back. He gestured for Clarinda to enter. She moved passed him and into the room. She bowed to Zebulon as the steward closed the door behind her.

"Have a seat," Zebulon said. Clarinda straightened up before moving to sit down in the chair. She looked around the office. The amount of books seemed to surprise her.

"What can I help you with?" Zebulon asked.

"I wanted to thank you for helping me get away from Blaine Breton this morning." Clarinda answered, "I did not expect anyone to help since my father had not seen me being taken away."

"He might have noticed if you have screamed," Zebulon said.

"Blaine promised to put a knife into my ribs if I made any noise that would attract attention." Clarinda said, "I was too scared to do anything but what he told me. Otherwise I would have screamed."

"I see," Zebulon said, "that is unfortunate."

"I expected him to show up again and try again, but I have not seen him," Clarinda said.

"I suggested to him that he might find a source of interest elsewhere," Zebulon said.

"Thank you for that." Clarinda said, "I appreciate it a lot."

"This may sound callus but it all comes with an ulterior motive," Zebulon said.

"And what is that?" Clarinda asked.

"It has been suggested to me several times over the last couple days that you would make a good choice for me to marry." Zebulon answered, "As much as you may not be my first choice in the matter, it seems the better choice."

"I see," Clarinda said. She was not as nervous anymore. Zebulon knew that this was much more her territory than his.

"However, any chance of marriage comes with conditions," Zebulon said.

"What conditions?" Clarinda asked.

"The first being that you must produce an heir before you take up with your lovers again." Zebulon answered, "The second is that the role of queen has the same amount of power when you hold it as it did for my mother, which is as an advisor when asked, but otherwise only over your own servants. And third that you keep any activity with your lovers private. I do not wish for any of it to be folder for the gossips in court. Do you have any problems with these conditions?"

"No, but I have some questions," Clarinda said.

"Go ahead," Zebulon replied.

"Our wedding will be planned by whom?" Clarinda asked.

"You with the help of anyone you need," Zebulon answered.

"Will we be sharing bed chambers?" Clarinda asked.

"No," Zebulon answered, "The ones across the hall from my room will be redecorated to your approval and that will be where you will sleep."

"And if I do not produce a son?" Clarinda asked.

"Then a daughter will take the throne." Zebulon answered, "She will be taught to rule Proster as I was taught by my father. The gender of the child matters less than that there is one."

"I see." Clarinda said, "I accept the proposition."

"Good." Zebulon said, "I will not make you sign a contract to those terms because I trust that you will obey them without it. I request however, that you wait for me to announce our engagement."

"I will not tell anyone until you have," Clarinda said.

"Good." Zebulon said, "You are dismissed."

Clarinda got up and left the officer. She closed the door on her way out.

Zebulon went back to the pile of paperwork.

It was time for supper when Zebulon had the pile finished. Halfway through that Herwin had brought the reports from the lower court for the day and Zebulon went through those as well. Now that the pile was finished, Zebulon got up and left his office. He went to the dining room, where supper was being served. He sat down at his spot and was given a plate of supper.

Zebulon was just about finished when the castle steward came to the table and bowed to him.

"Yes?' Zebulon asked after swallowing what was in his mouth.

"There is a messenger here from Jagel," the castle steward said.

"I will meet him in the throne room in five minutes," Zebulon said.

"Yes, Your Majesty," the castle steward bowed and left.

Zebulon finished his meal before leaving the dining room to head to the throne room. He arrived to find the messenger sitting on a chair resting. The messenger jumped to his feet when he saw Zebulon and bowed.

"Yes?" Zebulon asked. The messenger straightened up.

"The king of Jagel is appreciative of the letter that was sent about his diplomat Myles." the messenger said, "He said to tell you that Myles had been sent here because he as in debt to some men that were not pleasant people. Myles being his brother-in-law, the king did not want to see him killed over the debt. Thus the king sent him here as a diplomat. He figures that Myles ran out of money within the first month and that was why he had no money to pay the compensation. However, since Myles is now married and cannot go back to Jagel the king is able to be of an easier mind. Now he does not have to worry about what will happen when Myles gets back."

"I am glad he appreciates the situation," Zebulon said, "because I do not think Myles's wife's father was quite as happy."

"The other thing is that the king sent a treaty and the request that you send back a reply," the messenger said taking out a scroll from his bag and offering it to Zebulon. Zebulon took it.

"Go find some supper while I read it over," Zebulon said, "then you can go back with it tonight."

"Yes, Your Majesty," the messenger said. He bowed and then left the throne room following the smell of food.

Zebulon broke the seal and unrolled the scroll. The treaty the king of Jagel was offering was very similar to the one Zebulon had signed with Wodend. There was nothing in it that Zebulon disagreed with. He took it to his office and signed it. Then he found Herwin still in the lower court.

"What can I do for you, King Zebulon?" Herwin asked as he put down his quill.

"A treaty between us and Jagel." Zebulon answered, "It has a second place for a signature and I need you to sign it so that it can be sent back."

"Should this not go before the court?" Herwin asked.

"The one I signed with Wodend did not go before the court." Zebulon said, "Why should this one?"

"May I read it before I sign it?" Herwin asked.

"Certainly," Zebulon said handing the scroll to Herwin. Herwin took it and unrolled it. He read it over before picking up the quill and signing his name in the space provided.

"I do not see anything that will be a problem," Herwin said handing the scroll back to Zebulon.

"Neither did I," Zebulon said as he took the scroll. Zebulon left the lower court. Then he went back to the throne room. The messenger was back. He had obviously eaten and he had been given food for the trip back.

"Here is the treaty," Zebulon said offering the scroll back to the messenger. The messenger took it and put it away in his bag.

"Thank you, Your Majesty," the messenger said, "Thank you for the supper."

"You are welcome," Zebulon said. The messenger bowed again and then left the throne room. Zebulon turned and watched him leave. Then Zebulon headed up to his own bed chambers for the night.

Zebulon sat there while Lord Lodovico gave a report on the current state of the farms in Proster. As per his recent resolution, Zebulon tried not to fall asleep, but it was hard. Lord Lodovico droned on in detail about farming. Some of the other people in court were actually starting to look bored. Several times now it looked like he was wrapping it up, but then he went on.

Zebulon started to space out and his mind wandered to the sword lessons that Loic had offered for this afternoon. Zebulon's father had tried to teach him to use a sword, but Zebulon was more interested in books at that time. He made learned the basics to appease his father, but then given it up. Now he was ready to learn the rest. And no one was going to mock him in anyway. They learned that he could win a fight.

Herwin cleared his throat. Lord Lodovico stood there and looked expectantly at Zebulon.

"Thank you, Lord Lodovico for your report," Zebulon said.

"You are welcome," Lord Lodovico bowed and then left the throne room.

"Any other business?" Zebulon asked as the court slowly shook itself out of its slumber.

"There is some news of Lord Gwilym," Herwin said.

"What news it is?" Zebulon said.

"He died two days ago." Herwin said, "He left behind a country estate and a house in the city, but refused to name an heir after his son died. The messenger who brought the news said that there is no one prepared to take the position, though the estate will run smooth whether there is a lord there or not."

"But it needs a new lord," Zebulon said.

"Yes, Sire," Herwin said, "and soon."

"And your suggestion?" Zebulon asked.

"I have none at the moment," Herwin answered.

"I do." Zebulon said, "Dard, come forward."

Dard came forward and stopped in front of the dais. He bowed before looking up at Zebulon.

"For services rendered to the crown, I give you the title and property of Lord Gwilym," Zebulon said.

"Thank you, Your Majesty." Dard said and bowed, "I will use it to serve the crown."

"You will have to go out to the estate to check on it within the week," Zebulon said.

"I cannot get there until next week at the earliest," Dard said, "but I will go as soon as I can."

"Why can you not go until next week?" Zebulon asked.

"I have asked for Lady Thalia's hand in marriage and she has accepted." Dard answered, "We are to be married this week."

"Congratulations on your engagement and upcoming wedding." Zebulon said, "I hope both you and your bride enjoy your visit to the country estate."

"Thank you, Your Majesty," Dard said with a bow. He moved back into the crowd and Zebulon saw Thalia waiting for him. He suppressed the smile that wanted to come to his lips.

"Is there any further business?" Zebulon asked.

"Not that I know of, Your Majesty," Herwin answered. No one else spoke up when Zebulon looked over the group.

"Then there is one more announcement before the court is dismissed for the day," Zebulon said. Zebulon paused. Everyone was awake now and looking surprised by him having an announcement that was not prompted by Herwin. They waited for him.

"As of yesterday, Lady Clarinda and I are engaged," Zebulon announced. Everyone in court started applauding as Clarinda was pushed toward the front. She looked uncertain about it, but she was not being given an option.

Zebulon stood up and offered her his hand. She took it and stepped up on the dais with him. He put his arm around her waist and they faced the court. They both smiled as the people cheered.

"The court is dismissed for today," Zebulon said then the crowd quieted down. Zebulon let Clarinda go and she stepped down off the dais. People started coming up to her and congratulating her. She accepted it all with a smile, but there was some nervousness in her eyes.

Since there was no one else in the court who looked at her as if they wanted her dead, Zebulon figured that everything would be all right. In a couple days, Clarinda would be back to herself and her head would be held high with the fact that she was going to become queen. She had managed to get the king when no one else could get his attention. As long as she was not around every day asking him what he thought of this or that about the wedding. She could have whatever she wanted for a wedding as long as it stayed within the appropriate budget constraints. The castle steward would tell her how much she could afford in the next few days. Zebulon did not care as long he got the son that Saint Lang had showed him. It was highly unlikely that Saint Lang would show him such an image if that was not what would happen.

The throne room emptied out with everyone leaving, even Herwin. Zebulon stayed there and let the quiet fill him. It was a nice break from the problems he had just dealt with and the problems that were coming up. After all a wedding was going to be a chaotic endeavour, even if he wanted to avoid being part of the planning.

"Are you ready?" Zebulon asked Dard as they sat in the room provided for them in the church.

"To be married to Thalia, yes." Dard answered, "For this wedding, no."

"You will do fine." Zebulon said, "All you have to do is stand there and pay enough attention to know when to say your piece, slip the ring on to her finger, and remember to keep the kiss short."

"And all you have to do is stand there until the rings are asked for." Dard said, "It does not seem hard to you."

"Clarinda has been busy planning her wedding." Zebulon said, "I have heard about everything she wants and all the traditions she wants to include. So, I have to do all that and act like I am happy about it. That makes what you are about to do easy."

"It would not be that bad." Dard said, "How many wedding traditions could there be in Proster?"

"She found a book full of wedding traditions from all over the place." Zebulon said, "And she has read it cover to cover. She keeps coming to me with this tradition or that tradition. I have had to tell her that large animals will not be part of the ceremony in any way. I have strongly suggested that large amounts of smaller animals would not be a good idea either."

"What about the vows?" Dard asked, "There some very strange vows out there."

"The vows are already written." Zebulon answered, "They are simple and fit the circumstances of the marriage without giving away why we are getting married. Clarinda had found the part of vows, but even she decided that none of them fit the situation."

"At least she agrees with you there," Dard said. Zebulon nodded.

There was a knock on the door of the room before an usher opened the door.

"They are ready for you," the usher said.

"Thank you," Dard said as he and Zebulon got to their feet. They headed into sanctuary.

Dard stepped to his place beside the priest and Zebulon stopped a few feet behind him. There was some whispering from the people already seated, but both men ignored it. Zebulon had left all his symbols of office back at the castle so that the main focus would be Dard and Thalia. There would still be people who would try to focus on Zebulon, but they were going to be disappointed. Zebulon had given them as the argument for not being Dard's groomsman, but Dard had waved that off and insisted that only Zebulon qualified for the role. Even Thalia said that the wedding would not be complete without Dard's best friend as groomsman. Zebulon finally agreed, but left being king back at the castle.

The organist started playing the wedding march. The crowd fell to a hush. The doors to the back were opened by two ushers. The maid of honour came through with a swirl of emerald fabric, which matched the other decorations. She scattered white rose petals as she walked down the aisle. The maid of honour was Thalia's best friend since childhood and her personal servant. The girl's name was Gail, if Zebulon remembered correctly. They had only met once and that was very briefly. She had been very shy.

Gail reached the steps and was careful going up them. If she stepped on her skirt she might have fallen, but navigated quite well. Once she was in her place, she turned to the door as did everyone else.

"All rise for the bride," the priest said. People rose to their feet and Thalia entered being escorted by her father. She was wearing a white dress of satin with lace highlights that included bead work. A veil came down over her face, but everyone could see her and she could see everyone. Happiness glowed from her and Zebulon felt envious for Dard. Dard had found his true love and was just about to marry her. That was the best thing in the world. The only thing holding Zebulon to this world was not love for Clarinda, but love for the image of a boy he held in his head.

Thalia reached the steps. Dard went to her.

"I give my blessings to this union," Thalia's father said as he handed Thalia's hand to Dard. Dard took it with a slight bow to Thalia's father. Dard escorted Thalia up the steps the rest of the way to the priest.

"Ladies and gentleman," the priest started, "We are all here to witness the union of this couple in matrimony. God teaches us of love. Love of parent, love of neighbours, and most important of all love of spouse. This final love is what we are celebrating today.

"O God, we come before you. Hand in hand, these two people are stepping out in faith. We, who are gathered here, ask that you would take this couple into your hands. Help them, O God, to keep firm in the commitments they are just about to make. Guide them, O God, as they become a family, as they each change through the years. May they be flexible as they are faithful to you. And God, help us all to be your hands if there be need. Strengthen, tenderly all of our commitments. Amen."

The crowd sat down in their seats. The priest waited for the shuffling to subside before continuing.

"Let me charge you both to remember, that your future happiness is to be found in mutual consideration, patience, kindness, confidence, and affection," the priest said, "Dard, it is your duty to love Thalia as yourself, provide tender leadership, and protect her from danger. Thalia, it is your duty to treat Dard with respect, support him, and create a healthy, happy home. It is the duty of each of you to find the greatest joy in the company of the other; to remember that in both interest and affection, you are to be one and undivided.

"I charge you both, as you stand in God's presence, to remember that love and loyalty alone will serve as the foundations of a happy and enduring home. If the solemn vows which you are about to make are kept permanently, and if you steadfastly seek to do the will of your God, your life will be full of peace and joy, and the home which you are establishing will abide through every change.

"Dard and Thalia, you have made a very serious and important decision in choosing to marry each other today. You are entering into a sacred covenant as life partners in God. The quality of your marriage will reflect what you put into nurturing this relationship. You have the opportunity to go forward from this day to create a faithful, kind, and tender relationship. We bless you this day. It is up to you to keep the blessings flowing each and every day of your lives together. We wish for you the wisdom, compassion, and constancy to create a peaceful sanctuary in which you can both grow in love.

"Dard, do you understand and accept this responsibility, and do you promise to do your very best each day to create a loving, healthy, and happy marriage?"

"Yes, I do," Dard answered.

" Thalia, do you understand and accept this responsibility, and do you promise to do your very best each day to create a loving, healthy, and happy marriage?" the priest asked.

"Yes, I do," Thalia answered.

"The rings," the priest said. Zebulon took them out of his pocket and handed them to the priest.

"Let us pray. Bless, O God, the giving and receiving of these rings. May Dard and Thalia abide in Thy peace and grow in their knowledge of Your presence through their loving union. May the seamless circle of these rings become the symbol of their endless love and serve to remind them of the holy covenant they have entered into today to be faithful, loving, and kind to each other. Dear God, may they live in Your grace and be forever true to this union. Amen."

The priest offered the first ring to Dard. Dard took it and Thalia's hand.

"Thalia, I take you to be my lawfully wedded wife," Dard said, "Before these witnesses I vow to love you and care for you as long as we both shall live. I take you, with all your faults and strengths, as I offer myself to you with all my faults and strengths. I will help you when you need help, and turn to you when I need help. I choose you as the person with whom I will spend my life." Dard slipped the wedding band on to Thalia's finger.

The priest offered the second ring to Thalia. Thalia took it and Dard's hand.

"I, Thalia, take you, Dard, to be my husband. To share the good times and hard times side by side. I humbly give you my hand and my heart as sanctuary of warmth and peace, and pledge my faith and love to you. Just as the circle is without end, my love for you is eternal. Just as it is made of incorruptible substance, my commitment to you will never fail. With this ring, I thee wed." Thalia slipped the wedding band on to Dard's finger.

"Because Dard and Thalia have desired each other in marriage, and have witnessed this before God and our gathering, affirming their acceptance of the responsibilities of such a union, and have pledged their love and faith to each other, sealing their vows in the giving and receiving of rings, I do proclaim that they are husband and wife in the sight of God and man. Let all people here and everywhere recognize and respect this holy union, now and forever," the priest said, "Dear God, thank you for this beautiful day. You have fulfilled the desire of our hearts to be together in this life. We pray that your blessing will always rest upon our home; that joy, peace and contentment would dwell within us as we live together in unity, and that all who enter our home may experience the strength of your love. God, help us to follow and serve you with an ever growing commitment because of our union. Guide us into greater love and sacrifice as we care for each other's needs, knowing you will care for us. May we always be as keenly aware of your presence as we sense it today on our wedding day. And may our devotion in marriage be a radiant reflection of your love for us. Amen. You may kiss the bride."

Thalia helped Dard lift the veil over her head, which took some work with the weight of it. Then Dard did what he was told and kissed the bride.

"Ahh, true love," Saint Lang's voice said in Zebulon's ear, "Is that not sweet?" Zebulon could not agree more.

CONCLUSION?

Mitchell set the book down on the table beside him. He looked into the fire place. It was down again and if he was going to continue reading he would have to put another log on the fire. The sounds of the house were the only noises because the rest of the household had gone to bed. He should go to bed as well, but he sat there. There were books in that box and the next called to him to pick it up.

This book had been interesting. The suggestion that magic had been lost in the land and that magic users had left because of that. The problems of the demons and such were gone. It was still hard to believe that these books were anything but fiction. There were no records to support these as real. The government would very likely put Mitchell in prison if he brought these books out as real, even if the rest of the population would have laughed. But there was something about these books that suggested a truth. That and the fact that they had been hidden. If they were fiction, why hide them?

Mitchell got to his feet and picked up the book. He put the book back into the box. He should go to bed because he had a meeting the next day. Mitchell found himself picking up the next book and taking it over to the chair. He set the book on the table before putting the log on the fire. He sat down and made himself comfortable before picking up the book.

ABOUT THE AUTHOR

Heather Mantler is a lover of fairy tales and fables. She is also a student of psychology. She lives in Prince George, British Columbia and is a member of the writing group Scribblers Unanimous. Heather is always working on another story as she hopes to finish every story idea that she has ever written down. She was a nominee for the fiction category of the 2012 Prince George Regional Arts and Cultural Awards.

Heather encourages all her readers to post their reviews on Amazon.com or Good Reads.

www.ingramcontent.com/pod-product-compliance
Lightning Source LLC
Chambersburg PA
CBHW051513170626
46811CB00002B/799